HEROES of WARS

MEN FROM THE FUTURE

VIRAT VILAS PAWAR

Become Shakespeare
.com

First published in 2019 by

Becomeshakespeare.com

Wordit Content Design & Editing Services Pvt Ltd
Unit - 26, Building A-1, Nr Wadala RTO, Wadala (East),
Mumbai 400037, India
T:+91 8080226699

©
ISBN - 978-93-88942-08-9

Disclaimer

This novel is heavily inspired from the world's greatest Epic : Mahabharat.

All the characters and incidents in this Novel are imaginary, resemblance to any person dead or alive is purely coincidental. The writer does not intend to outrage, insult, wound or hurt any religion or the religious sentiments, beliefs or feelings of any person(s) or class or community.

This is pure fiction and for people to enjoy the idea of mythology with a science fiction twist to it.

About The Author

Virat Vilas Pawar born 15th July 1995 is a BMM graduate and currently pursuing law. Virat is a true passionate millennial who believes in expanding his horizons. This multitasker also runs a Digitial Marketing Agency called Epitome Media And Management.

A sci-fi buff since childhood, he put his passion into words and Heroes of Wars- Men From Future was born. A rare combination of Mythology and science fiction, a story heavily inspired by the greatest epic- Mahabharat.

He plans to turn this into a trilogy and give India something new and exciting!

You can connect with him on -
Email : viratpawar10@gmail.com
Instagram : viratvilaspawar.docx

Acknowledgment

I believe India is a treasure of mythology. Any character from the epics can be picked up and turned into a superhero arch. Talking about heroes, I want to thank the heroes without whom this book wouldn't be possible.

I want to start with my parents, Dr. Vilas Jairam Pawar and Mrs. Vishakha Vilas Pawar for being so supportive from the day I discussed this idea with them. Without their blessing, this project would have never begun.

My editor Nibedita Nandi, who gave countless hours for editing and creating a better version of my story; I am ever grateful to her for supporting me in my dream project. Aditi Gandhi for stepping in at the last moment and doing the golden polish with her editing skills. Thanks to Manisha Thakur ma'am for the final proof reading. Thanks to Sameer Amblidhok from BecomeShakespeare.com (the publishers) for being so co-operative till the last moment.

A big thanks to Shiladitya Bose and Shubhadeep Roy who gave their heart and soul while spending innumerable sleepless nights and turning my imagination into marvellous characters. I also want to thank Siddharth Thampi, who created the logos of F.A.T.E and Heroes of Wars, another artist I am fortunate to have come across. Big shout out to my Team Epitome Media and Management who supported me with the Digital Marketing for the book. Special shout out to Sanish Kulkarni who designed the creatives for the social media campaigns.

Without these guys, Heroes of Wars: Men From Future would have been just a file in the E Drive of my laptop.

At last, the most important, I would like to thank you, my readers. I hope you enjoy my alternate version of the greatest epic of all times.

Thank you.

Contents

Prologue

A great war just came to an end, a war that involved things beyond anyone's imagination. Kison stood in the middle of the war zone wearing his golden battle armour which looked unharmed and shined bright, not a single bruise on his blue tinted skin. A gentle wind wiped away the single drop of sweat that ran down his face, the peacock feather that decorated his headgear waved along with the blow. Kison looked at his chariot that was broken into pieces. He looked around him and all he could see was death and destruction. Dead bodies, dead elephants, horses, people with 100 arrows pierced into their bodies, slit throats and dismembered bodies. The soil had turned red with the blood of the fallen. A sight one could never forget, a sight Kison had to remember for the rest of his life.

"I couldn't stop it!" he whispered in disgrace.

"I have to fix this, I will fix this. I will try again!" he exclaimed as he clenched his fists, and looked towards the sky with anger, frustration, but mostly shame.

He screamed and in that very moment, there was a flash of light across the sky.

Somewhere else...

Kison stood in a dark room, a small oil lamp was placed at a distance. Hardly anything was visible in that room. He kept looking around to find something familiar. He looked above him and saw many temple bells. He could smell joss sticks; the aroma calmed him down. It looked like a Hindu Temple. There was a huge window with a view of the entire city. He walked towards the window and found the place where he was standing was on top of the tallest building. He peeped outside to get a better view and witnessed hovering cars and people riding on creatures that he had not seen in his world. He looked further and noticed a building being robbed and many more crimes happening.

"What brought you here Kison?" a female voice asked from the other end of the room.

Kison didn't utter a word. He just hung his head in shame.

"You failed again, didn't you?" the voice whispered.

"Yes"

"You cannot fix the inevitable Kison. What's done is done!"

"If I wanted to, I could have stopped it. I should learn something from you. You saved the entire world. You are the reason why this world is still alive, Kalki," Kison said with his head still hung in shame.

Kalki came out of the darkness. Her eyes glowed, it

wasn't just her hair that hovered but she was 3 inches off the floor. She was the epitome of beauty- she looked weak and her skin had slight wrinkles- and her grace was unmatched, her glowing eyes made her look ethereal. She wore a white saree that had golden embroidery across, also, a peacock feather was hanging on the necklace she wore. The saree looked dusty but it was well draped. Kalki had beautiful lips and a sharp nose. She didn't look like an ordinary woman.

"I wasn't alone Kison, I had to take help from Guru Saheb, Prophet Ali, and Chris. We managed to stop the destruction of the world but at what cost? I lost them, it wasn't even their war. I came here to save the world, but I couldn't do that," she whispered as she looked outside the giant window.

"Still the world lives, the humans breathe," Kison replied.

"My purpose of recreating the world couldn't be fulfilled, our job was to destroy the Adharma, but if I had to do that, it meant I had to let the destruction of the world happen. And after me, there was no one who would raise the humanity. I am the last one," Kalki said as she walked near the window.

"We can change this, I need your help. We can stop this Kalki," Kison said as he walked towards her.

"And how exactly are you planning to do that?" she inquired.

"Give me five of your best men from this world. Let them fight the war of Kurukshetra, let's win the war and let's change this ugly future," he replied.

Listening to this, Kalki quickly turned around, "The rules of time travel are no different for us Kison"

"I know, but this is the only way to rebuild the world and stop this future. You don't have to go through the eternal pain and the other Gods don't have to die," he said, as he looked into the glowing eyes of Kalki.

"How does it feel to manipulate your future self, Kison?" she muttered.

"I have no options left. I have tried infinite possibilities and now this is all I have got," he replied as he looked away trying to avoid looking into her eyes directly.

"I hope you are aware that you want to change the events of the past, past that took place thousands of years ago. Past that has important layers of present and future on it, right?" she asked him.

Kison nodded.

"That means if you succeed, everything that happened after you till today will be wiped out and a whole new world will be formed," she said as she landed on the floor.

"Yes!" Kison replied.

"Kison! If that happens, the ugly future will be saved but another future will take place which we haven't designed, which we haven't foreseen or where we will have no idea what to do. Are you prepared for that?" she asked him in distress.

"What are the odds? At least we can try," Kison said, looking more like a helpless human than a God.

"I am tired of providing energy to this world. I am exhausted of balancing the universe. This is our last shot. If we fail, everything our incarnations have done so far will fail and the world will cease to exist. But I am willing to take this chance," she said as she raised her hands.

"I won't disappoint you or anyone else," he replied.

Kalki raised her hands in the air and a huge light came from behind her.

"Don't let your efforts be just another ripple in the sea of time, may you cause a tide. You have my word, you will get the best five from my era to protect yours and do the impossible. With this, there will be other branches that will come out in the tree of time and it's your responsibility to do the needful," she said as her voice faded away.

Force Against Terror and Extraterrestrials

F.A.T.E.

Chapter 1.

F.A.T.E.

– Force Against Terror and Extra-Terrestrials.

Year: 3025

Location: F.A.T.E. Headquarters.

Time: 3:35 AM

Nakul was sleeping in his bed, wearing matching pajamas, when suddenly a gadget of which the screen was placed up-side down on the table, besides his bed chimed.

"No, Please! I don't wanna eat tomatoes," he yelled out as he woke up with a jerk.

He looked at the gadget and muttered, "Oh, just a dream. Phew! I despise tomatoes, man!" and he picked up the gadget to check what had interrupted his nightmare of tomatoes.

He touched a button, and a hologram popped out of the gadget and projected a man's silhouette.

"Report to the mission room in next 5 minutes..."

He looked at the clock that displayed the time as 3:36 AM.

"Man, they really got to have some regards for people's

off duty hours," he said as he stretched his fatigued body and got off the bed.

As soon as he stepped his foot on the ground, it illuminated with soft light. He had a badge on his right chest that looked like a part of him. He double tapped it and semi-solid particles rushed out of the badge. They looked like tiny black pebbles that were soft and sticky yet firm. Within a second, they covered his body, and his night clothes turned into a black skin suit. It was tailored perfectly to accentuate his physique and also protect it, with heavy padding around the knees, elbows, and shoulders. It made him look battle ready. The badge glowed with the sigil of 'F.A.T.E.'

He walked towards his locker and pulled out a drawer. As he opened it, there was a small container that had finely crushed crystals in it. He looked at it for a moment and forcefully shut the drawer. He left with a huge sigh.

Nakul walked to the door and it automatically opened, he marched towards the mission room. The lights in the hallway were dim; each of them got brighter as he walked past the previous one. He walked in a rather funny manner and hummed his favourite song.

Nakul seemed like a very carefree and happy person. He believed in enjoying each moment with a constant smile along with a twinkle in his eyes. He was a handsome fellow with features that could match a God. His pale white skin, perfect jaw, and nose could mesmerize anyone. His spiked hair looked alluring with his strong face.

Soon he reached the mission room and noticed that

Bheem and Deva were already present over there. Both of them wore the same suit as Nakul.

Bheem looked at Nakul and said, "You are late."

"Yeah man, I took a few seconds to recover from my nightmare of tomatoes," he said as he walked towards Bheem.

Bheem had a muscular body, unlike Deva and Nakul his body wasn't fully covered, his suit was more like a vest. His huge muscular biceps and the cuts on it were easily visible. He had a body like a bull, enhanced by his height and broad shoulders. His dreadlocks reached his muscular back, and he had the perfect French beard that suited his jawline. Although dusky, his skin was smooth and beautiful.

Deva, on the other hand, was skinny and short. He was the tech guy. He was a nerd, but they loved him for it. He was holding a cube in his hand that projected information in the form of a holograph. Deva had drooping shoulder and a hump in his back. The dark circles around his eyes clearly meant that he worked late hours and focused very less on his fitness.

A huge screen lit up, and the man's silhouette appeared again.

"Alright warriors! There is a situation which has to be addressed urgently, I have sent the mission details on your badge, you can check it out on your way. However, I would like to inform you that this is a tough mission and has to be executed immediately."

Deva tapped his badge which was on the right side of his chest, promptly a holograph projection was in front of him.

It displayed :

'Mission Details:

Mafia Ruban is smuggling forty-six hundred kilos of liquid helium.

A convoy of 5 fully equipped hovering trucks and five levitating bikes are providing utmost protection.

Extract the helium and arrest Ruban, unharmed.

Location: Sector 400610'

"Isn't that Yudhraj's territory? Shouldn't we inform him?" Deva prompted.

"No! Do not involve him, this is a covert operation and nobody should know about this," the man on the screen instantly commanded.

"Alright people! Let's do this!" Nakul screamed with enthusiasm.

Before anybody could move, the man on the screen continued "However, there is a small complication. Mafia Ruban has a bounty of Rs.45 crores on his head..."

"No, don't say it, please don't say it," Nakul interrupted even before the man could finish his sentence.

"Yes, he has a bounty on his head, and our ex-warrior Arjun has taken up the contract," he continued.

"Scammy Kammy! We are screwed," Nakul exclaimed.

"So what is our primary mission?" Bheem asked.

"Your mission is to locate Mafia Ruban, extract the helium from him, stop Arjun from killing him, and bring Arjun to the headquarters."

Suddenly Nakul laughed out hysterically.

"I would rather eat tomatoes. No way the three of us can capture that maniac. We need a force to execute this mission. Forget the mission, we need a force just to trap Arjun, let alone locating the mafia and extracting the helium from his tight security," and continued laughing.

Deva, who was engrossed in his deep thoughts, broke the chain of his calculations and instantly said, "Where is Karan? Shouldn't we have him if we are going against Arjun? I mean it's not a good option to have a mongoose and snake fight, but practically speaking this is a very complicated mission."

The man on the screen left a sigh and said, "I am aware, but Karan has not returned from his previous mission yet. He will be joining you shortly. Also, do not engage Karan with Arjun. I don't want destruction in that peace-loving sector governed by Yudhraj."

Bheem cracked his knuckles as he heard the man

"Alright team. We got to hold the fort until Karan arrives. Let's go," he said.

Everyone turned around in sync, and suddenly some rock and roll music faded in.

"What's that?" Bheem asked as he was surprised to hear the music.

Both of them looked at Nakul who was playing a song on his device.

"Man, we need a good background score for such moments, this seems appropriate," he said as he grooved to the drums.

Bheem ignored him and everyone walked out.

Sector 400610:

It was still dark; the sun had not graced its presence yet. A man sat on the edge of a tall building, monitoring something with his advanced binoculars. He spotted a convoy of 5 trucks far away from his location within a few moments. He pressed a button and the binoculars retracted into a small frame.

He got up and flexed his muscles. His body was agile and strong. He was wearing a white and grey armour. His gloves had some heavy mechanism and looked like something could pop out of it. In the centre of his palm, he had a horizontal handle and a button right next to it. He pressed the button, and a bow retracted out of his glove. It was a foldable bow that he could carry anywhere. A bow without a string.

He too had a badge of 'F.A.T.E.' on his right chest, but the sigil was scribbled off. He tapped the badge, raised his right hand and clenched his fist. He looked at it, and the semi-solid particles came out of the badge and covered his right hand. In moments it started glowing and emitting bright blue light as if his arm had turned into a thunderbolt. Its glow broke the darkness of the night.

He placed his bow in front of him and brought his shining hand near the bow. As soon as his hand came near the bow, a string made out of energy came out and connected both the limbs of the bow, he pulled the string. As he did so, an arrow was produced out of the bright blue energy. The arrow was emitting the same energy as his right hand. He gripped the bow, moved it towards the sky, dragged the string and shot the arrow. A ripple was caused in the air as the arrow was shot. The arrow paced at the speed of light, illuminating the sky. It went and hit one of the trucks from the convoy and caused a huge blast.

All the other trucks stopped instantly.

A dozen men wearing advanced armour and holding guns came out of one truck and surrounded the small vehicle that contained the liquid helium. The smoke cleared.The same man was standing in front of them. The heavily armed men moved a step back as they saw the man with his lightning arm staring right at them.

"I don't want to cause any harm, I need the helium and also the head of your boss. Let me have it, and we can leave peacefully," he said in a calm voice.

The door of the vehicle opened, and a fat man stepped out. He was bald and wore a white three-piece suit. The infamous Mafia Ruban.

"Oh, Arjun! I saw this coming, but unfortunately, you aren't getting either of the things you demanded," Mafia Ruban said.

"Alright then, let's do it my way," Arjun said as he raised his bow.

"OPEN FIRE!" the mafia exclaimed and jumped back into his car.

All the heavily armed guards started shooting laser beams towards Arjun.

He sprang from his position and ran to take cover.

Within no time a dozen more heavily armed men gathered to shoot him down.

He peeped to understand how many men he had to shoot. He dodged the lasers and bolted towards the other side of the street while firing his energy arrows towards the men. The arrows caused a lot of damage to the men and the surrounding, but that wasn't enough. He decided to move but realised that he was cornered by the men. He steadily got up, and his arm stopped glowing.

"Put your bow down," an armed man said.

"Can't!" he replied.

"Everybody fire!" the armed man exclaimed.

All of them pulled their trigger at once and innumerable lasers were blasted towards Arjun.

Suddenly someone plunged in front of him, and Arjun was unharmed.

He saw a tall and perfectly built man stood in front of him, holding a shield made out of energy. The dust cleared, and Arjun saw that the man threw something on the ground; small fragments broke out of it that bounced straight towards the armed men, electrocuting them and causing them to fall on the ground, grunting in pain.

He pressed a button on his wrist, and the shield went off, he looked back at Arjun and said-

"Dare you cause any disturbance in my territory."

Arjun looked at him as he saw him looking straight into his eye.

"I could have handled it. Your assistance wasn't needed Yudhraj."

Yudhraj was the governor of this sector. The most deserving candidate, a person who topped the Community Leadership Program of F.A.T.E. and became the ruler of one of the biggest sectors in the world. There was something about him that made him look royal, definitely not the looks but the vanity he possessed. His fair skin and blue eyes added to the essence, his wavy hair defined his supremacy.

"Yes, I could see that," Yudhraj said as he looked at the armed men lying on the ground.

Before Yudhraj could say anything else, Arjun hurtled towards the mafia.

"This man won't listen," Yudhraj muttered and ran after Arjun to stop him from causing any more damage.

Arjun tapped his badge, and his arm lit up again, as he pulled the string of his bow and shot another energy arrow towards the vehicle, where the mafia was hiding.

The door exploded, and the mafia fell on the ground!

Arjun pointed the energy arrow towards him and said, "There are two options, either you tell me where the liquid helium is and then I kill you or first I will kill you and then find it. The choice is yours."

"You think I came unprepared?" the mafia asked with a grin on his face and quickly pressed a button on his watch.

As soon as he pressed the button, many armed robots popped out of one of the trucks.

Arjun saw this and sprinted back towards Yudhraj.

"Now might be a good time for you to actually help me," Arjun said as he unclasped his bow and tapped his badge.

"Sure!" Yudhraj said as he retracted his sword and shield made out of energy.

They both moved and stood in front of the army of armed robots.

Arjun heard a loud whooshing sound behind him, he looked up in the sky and saw a ship approaching them. A spotlight was projected over both of them.

"Need some help?" Nakul announced from the P.A. of the ship.

He placed the mic back in its place and looked at Bheem.

"Can I please do a superhero landing, please?"

Bheem left a sigh and said,

"Do whatever you want but do something," and he opened the base door of the ship.

Nakul with a broad smile ran towards the base door and jumped out, he did a dramatic landing with his right knee on the ground and stood up in slow motion.

"How much would you rate that?" he asked with his eyes opened wide out of enthusiasm to get in combat.

Followed by that even Bheem jumped casually on the ground, as he jumped, everyone felt a slight tremor. He held an advance mace in his hand, instead of the globe it had a cylindrical top which was made out of the same energy as that of Yudhraj's shield.

Everyone ignored Nakul's question as Bheem passed by him.

He looked at Yudhraj and said, "Sorry for the destruction caused; the organization will take care of it."

Deva chose to stay on the ship, providing them insights and a bird's eye view of the entire situation.

All four of them were ready to fight the armed robots. Bheem took the lead and charged towards the robots while swinging his mace. Even before others could attack, he thwacked the robots into scrap with his mace.

He did the optimum utilization of his muscle power.

With a lot of zeal, Nakul stabbed the robots with his

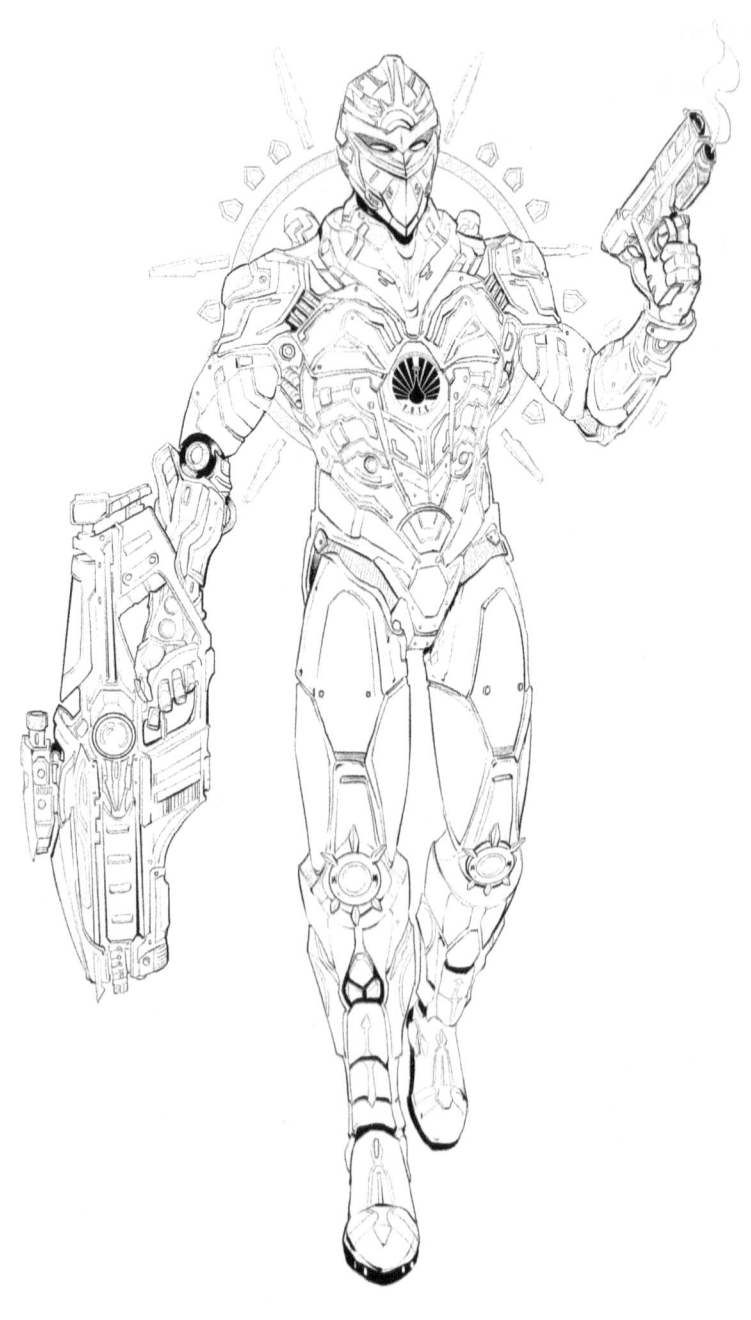

spear. The head of the spear had a red colour rare crystal that had sharp edges which made it look majestic.

After a brief fight when dozens of robots turned into trash, all of them stopped to catch their breath. They stood in a circle with their backs to each other.

The first ray of the sun hit the ground, making everything visible.

The number of robots that came towards them didn't stop.

Bheem looked at the ship, touched his coms that were placed in his left ear, and said, "Deva! I think you should inform the headquarters and call for back-up."

Arjun approached the robots and shot each one of them with arrows; he didn't know the word 'stop.' He was at the peak of his stamina and power.

Suddenly a huge sonic wave was shot from the sky that destroyed half of the robots.

Everyone looked at the sky and saw someone diving down. He came down with great speed, while he glided down, he had a hologram projecting from his back that looked like the sun. He landed straight on his feet effortlessly. Everyone looked at him as his golden mask shrunk down into an ear piece, making his face visible.

"Karan! My man!" Nakul exclaimed.

Karan was the personification and epitome of perfection. He wore a bright golden armour that covered his entire body. The armour had golden light running across it that looked like energy. Karan's smart looks were unmatched, his physical features were incomparable. He looked like the best of God's creations. As he stood, the holograph of the sun behind his back made him look even more majestic.

Karan and Arjun shared a glance, for a second they forgot everything and stared into each other's eyes with rage, they shared a look like that of sworn enemies. It seemed like they would leave everything aside and have a hand to hand amongst themselves.

"Focus!" Yudhraj screamed out.

"I want this mess out of my sector," he added.

With a collective effort, they managed to destroy the army of robots; the entire road turned into scrap as Yudhraj looked around.

"Should have come sooner," Bheem said as he looked at Karan.

"Sorry! I had to travel across the galaxy to finish a mission. I am not as lucky as you guys who get to beat up tin men," Karan replied as he mocked the team.

"Wait! Where is he? Where is Arjun?" Karan asked as he looked around in distress.

Karan noticed that Arjun was driving away the truck that contained the liquid helium. He ran towards the truck that had almost gained momentum. As the truck took a little speed, Karan dived right in front of it. Arjun, instead of applying breaks, accelerated towards him.

Karan stood in front of the truck with his chest out, the

truck bashed into Karan, but he remained unharmed. The armour he wore was so strong that the impact caused no harm to him, instead the truck's bonnet was crushed. The impact had knocked out Arjun.

Karan pulled him out of the truck and cuffed him.

He dragged Arjun where the rest of them were standing, "Alright! Let's go to the headquarters."

They safely collected the liquid helium and transported it to the headquarters.

Mission Room:

The screen turned on, and the same man appeared on the screen.

"Good job team," he congratulated everyone.

"Arjun, you are about to be imprisoned for a very long time under every possible charge," he added.

"You think the security of the F.A.T.E can hold me?" Arjun said with his chin thrust out while he was on his knees and his hands were cuffed behind his back.

The man took a pause and said, "Karan! You have to deliver this helium to Sector 59 facility of F.A.T.E. and come back to report to me. You will depart immediately."

"Yes Sir!" Karan roared and prepared to leave the room. Before he could leave the room, he looked back at Arjun and coldly said, "When I come back I will personally attend to you," and the door shut automatically.

The man cleared his throat. Only his silhouette was visible on the screen.

"Attention everyone! I have a mission for you. This is the biggest task assigned to us in the history of F.A.T.E. A mission where nothing can go wrong. No questions to be asked, only orders are to be followed. This is a mission that I have been asked to execute by the supreme authority," he said.

Everyone listened carefully to what the man on the screen said.

"Uncuff Arjun," he commanded.

Yudhraj narrowed his eyes and said, "But sir!"

"I said, only orders to be followed."

"Arjun! We have got a tip about the whereabouts of Abhimanyu," the man said in a very serious tone.

Arjun gasped as he heard the name Abhimanyu, it got back all his attention as he stood on his feet.

"Do not stoop so low that you have to bring in my dead son," Arjun yelled at the screen.

"Arjun, even you don't know for sure if he is dead or alive, but I have got a piece of information which might be helpful for you."

"How do I even trust you? This whole organization runs on a flawed system, and since Dronaji and Bhishmaji are gone, I wonder how all this is still running. Fate my foot!" Arjun exclaimed.

"You can get your son back, Arjun," the man said, ignoring him.

"If you want my services, simply pay me. I shall do it but don't talk about my dead son," Arjun repeated.

The screen got divided into half, and a photo of a young boy was displayed on the screen, it wasn't clear, but it was detailed enough to moist Arjun's eye.

Yudhraj placed his hand on Arjun's shoulder,

"This is good news, we can find him. Don't worry," assuringly, he comforted.

With his moist eyes, he looked back at Yudhraj.

The screen changed to what it was earlier and the man continued.

"This is an inter-dimension mission; you have to travel to a different dimension, probably a different time zone. This is a primitive era and all of you will have to participate in the mission. Everyone will be rewarded heavily and also with the ranks," the man said.

"Yudhraj, we would like to hire your services as you still belong to F.A.T.E. Your sector will be looked after by our security," he added.

Yudhraj gazed at Arjun who was suffering from mixed emotions and quickly looked back at the screen.

"You have been given an order not a choice," the man said in a sharp voice.

"Yes sir!" Yudhraj exclaimed.

Nakul who wasn't expected to stay quiet for too long interrupted and said,

"You mean we are gonna time travel? That is so freaking cool!"

The man on the screen continued.

"I hope everyone is ready for the mission."

"But? What exactly is our mission?" Bheem inquired.

"You will get all the details, a man named Kison will be waiting for you at the Rendezvous point, your ship is equipped with platinum grade weapons and essentials. You have to depart immediately. All the best for the mission," the man said and the screen turned off.

Arjun was quiet as he remembered the picture of his son.

Yudhraj stood in front of them and said,

"Alright everyone! If we have been given a mission that is so important, we should execute it. It's not just about us anymore," he said as he looked at Arjun.

"Everyone, we will meet at the launch pad in 30 minutes!" he exclaimed.

Chapter 2.

KISON

The five men embarked on their journey towards the unknown. Arjun sat in his chamber near the window that displayed a splendid view of the space outside. He gazed at the shining stars and meteors that travelled at high speed. Arjun wasn't exactly staring at the marvellous colourful stars and moons; he was lost in deep thoughts. Thoughts of his son and his whereabouts played in his mind.

The door buzzed open and Yudhraj walked inside the chamber.

"I know this can be hard on you, but going to a mission without knowing anything about it is equally dangerous. We are not here just for credit points, but we all want Abhi to get back to you," Yudhraj said as he walked towards him.

"Yes, so that I can owe you all?" Arjun murmured as he still kept looking outside the window.

"I am here because of the promise that my sector will get allowances and will be given proper treatment. Nakul and Bheem are here because they have been ordered to do so. I am not enjoying this either, but we have to do what we have to."

Arjun didn't pay attention to what he said and got up.

"I don't need a pep talk as of now; we are heading towards a mission none of us have ever encountered. Let's save some energy for any unforeseen events. Okay?" Arjun said and signalled the door to open, implying Yudhraj to leave him alone.

"As you wish Arjun," Yudhraj said and left the chamber.

AFTER SOMETIME.

After traveling at enormous speed and several worm holes to travel across time, they finally reached a planet that looked like earth but much greener. The ship landed at the location, which was a dense forest, and it was pitch dark. As the ship approached the landing spot, heavy winds broke loose, and the temperate forest suddenly woke up. The winds seemed to calm down but the night seemed anything but. Wolves could be heard howling at a distance, and the sky was lit up with a million stars that only made the forest look more eerie and uninviting.

Everyone stood facing towards the exit. Arjun held a wooden bow in his hand and carried a quiver full of arrows.

Yudhraj looked at him and asked, "Going too old school?"

"Obviously! According to the mission report, I guess we are in the copper age, technology is far fetched for them. So the first rule of time travel is to 'blend'," Arjun replied as he adjusted the strap of his quiver.

Everyone tapped their badges, and their clothes turned into the black skin suits which had their sigils on it, except Arjun.

Yudhraj looked at Arjun's sigil and said "I see you have scribbled your sigil, too much hate towards the organization?"

"Not hate, Yudhraj, I don't hold any pride in being part of the academy anymore. Let's focus on the mission," he replied in a dry tone.

The ship's ramp slid out of the exit door and thudded on the ground, the door buzzed open, and the light from the chambers streamed out. The pale white light wasn't enough for them to clearly see their surroundings.

"Let me go first," Arjun said as he saw Yudhraj moving towards the door.

He nodded and let Arjun walk out.

Arjun walked out and carefully monitored everything possibly he could see in the dark, he was quiet and observant, he left no stone unturned while doing so.

"Clear," he exclaimed from the outside.

Listening to this, the remaining four came out as well.

As Nakul stepped out on the grass, he yelled out 'Fresh!'

He took a deep breath and added, "Man, this place is so pleasant. The air is so rich."

"Keep it low," Bheem muttered as he looked around.

There was a sudden movement in the nearby bushes; everyone heard it, ready to be engaged.

Arjun pulled an arrow out of his quiver, placed on his bow and stretched the string.

Kison walked out of the bushes; he was steady and looked at the five men.

Arjun pointed the arrow towards him and exclaimed, "Stand down."

Kison raised his hands in the air and said, "You are from F.A.T.E. if I am not wrong?"

As soon as Arjun heard the word fate, he lowered his bow.

Yudhraj approached him with a smile, "You must be Kison, we were asked to meet you. Hope we are on time."

Kison rested his hand, smiled back at Yudhraj, and said, "Time, time is a vague concept. The fact that you had to travel here means that you are too late, but the fact that I am meeting you states that you are on time."

Everyone had a confused look on their face as they heard him breaking the time travel theory.

Nakul approached Kison with his arms wide open and hugged him tightly, "Kison, my man! It's so nice to meet you. I know we are late, but I am glad we are on time! Please tell us what our task is."

Kison tried to free himself from the firm grip of Nakul.

"You must be Nakul?" Kison asked him.

"Oh, yes, I forgot to introduce myself. I am Nakul," He said with a wide smile.

"Allow me to introduce you to my buddies," he added. "To start with the guy who almost fired an arrow at you, his name is Arjun. The guy standing behind, yeah the guy who has a super duper muscular body is Bheem, the guy next to him is Deva, he looks malnourished but he just spends a lot of time researching and last but not the least, our royalty, our Highness, King Yudhraj," he introduced.

"I want to thank you all for coming on such short notice. I assume you had a long journey. You can rest here for the night, and we will meet tomorrow morning, is that fine by you all?" Kison inquired

Arjun looked at Kison and said, "Okay! We set camp here; this seems to be a perfect location for us to function. The river is 500 meters south from here and there are no dangerous animals around except for the porcupines that have their hubs behind the rocks that are 22 inches thick; these rocks should be around west 1 kilometre away from this spot, so we are safe. The closest human dwelling is two kilometres east away from here, but that seems like it's an empty house or just a single person stays there. The sun here sets in the east and the entire east patch is covered with thick, dense oak trees, so it's going to get dark quickly, that adds up to our advantage. So we set up here."

Kison smiled and thought, "Arjun, you never fail to impress."

Nakul looked at Arjun from a distance and said to himself, "Wish we had him at our thick and thin times,

Arjun being the kind of freak could have helped the organization so much," as he smiled.

"Alright then, you all can rest now, and we will gather tomorrow near the river."

Arjun nodded in agreement and everyone returned to the ship.

Kison left them as they prepared for the night; he walked towards the outskirts of the jungle only a short distance away from the ship into a small hut. It was his home. The shed was made of mud and had a stone roof. He got inside the house and sat on the hemp mattress that was on the floor.

He looked at the plain wall and said to himself, "What I am about to do is going to change everything. Everything has changed already. Regardless of the outcome, is it our victory or our defeat? Everything is changed now. I am not even sure if this is the right thing to do, but this one is for the future," soon he fell asleep with a heavy heart.

SUNRISE

That night everyone slept inside the ship.

Arjun was the first one to wake up. He picked up his bow and quiver and left the ship. It was foggy outside because of the cold; the sun was only partially visible from behind the enormous hills.

Soon he arrived at the river.

The water was reflecting the sun rays and looked

yellowish. Birds were chirping nearby. Everything was very scenic, unlike the night before.

Arjun stood there for a while as if waiting for something; he took a deep breath and said, "You don't have to spy on me Yudhraj," as he looked at the river.

Arjun looked back and saw Yudhraj getting out of the bushes nearby.

"I wasn't spying on you," he hesitated.

"I am not going to abandon you like I did last time; I am doing this for a reason. If there is even a slight chance that Abhi is still alive, I want to take it," Arjun said as he gazed at the ripples on the river.

"We will find him and you don't have to worry," Yudhraj replied in a low tone.

Yudhraj looked at Arjun and said, "Sometimes I envy you a lot Arjun. You have no rules, no regulations, a free man, a man of his own will. You don't have to report to anyone either. How does it feel after living a long life at F.A.T.E. and turning into a man like this?"

"There was a reason why I was a part of the organization; without that reason, I could no longer stay there. I had to do what I needed to do. I had to live and earn. I could have taken up any job, but I trained hard to gain my skills. My life has been hard on me, so I don't care how anyone else's life turns out to be after what I do to them," Arjun replied in a cold tone.

"If someone says they don't care, they are lying. We all

care about things, but the human inside us doesn't know to express," Yudhraj said in a mild tone.

Both of them were helpless in their ways, both had no options but to survive with whatever they had.

They both stood near the river bank and looked at the sun changing its color.

Arjun heard footsteps and saw Nakul, Bheem, and Deva walking towards them.

Kison helmed on his boat and stopped when it reached the bank. He swiftly jumped out of the boat and approached them.

"You are late, man," Nakul said.

"No! I was on time. I was securing the perimeter," Kison said as he looked at Nakul.

"So what do you want us to do now?" Bheem asked as he came forward.

"Let's start with a little friendly fight?" Kison said with a smile.

Bheem scoffed and looked at Yudhraj.

"So, who goes first?" Nakul asked with much enthusiasm.

Kison looked at him and replied, "All of you."

Deva was shocked "What? Whoever you might be or however strong you might be, you cannot fight all of us at the same time".

"Oh, Come on!" Kison said in his unassuming voice.

Bheem marched towards him with speed and punched him as hard as he could; Kison instantly blocked his punch with his forearm. As soon as Bheem's blow hit Kison's forearm, he was thrown back with an incredible force.

"Impossible!" exclaimed Deva with amazement and a little fear.

Nakul jumped towards Kison and attacked his legs, Kison backflipped and dodged Nakul's attack. He went a step back and saw Bheem was still trying to get up; he instantly jumped on Nakul and dropped a punch on his face. This made Yudhraj angry, he headed towards Kison, and both of them started a hand- to-hand combat. Kison punched him in the stomach and in return Yudhraj punched him in the face. Nakul charged back at him while Bheem was getting back to his senses. Kison jumped in the air and kicked Yudhraj.

Yudhraj fell a few feet away. And before Nakul could finish his attack, Kison caught him in mid-air with his hands and threw him down.

Kison nailed him against the ground and got up. As soon as he moved, Arjun's arrow came flying towards him and without even blinking he caught the arrow. Arjun was shocked. Kison threw the arrow back at him with thrust so intense that it was a blur. He quickly jumped and dodged the arrow.

"Alright, stop!" Deva exclaimed.

Everyone stood up, and Kison was standing in the center. All of them were breathing heavily.

Deva looked at Kison and said, "You proved your point. We figured you are stronger than all of us combined."

Kison stood there casually as he didn't even break a sweat.

Yudhraj walked towards Kison and said, "If you are so strong and know everything, then why did you call us here?"

Kison looked at him and said, "Because I cannot fight this war. If I do, it will do more damage to the future than it would do in your absence."

Deva tried to understand his cryptic words, while the others stood silently attempting to make sense of what had just happened.

Chapter 3
The Kingdom

"I can't speak of it, I cannot be part of this war and I cannot pick up a weapon against anyone in this war," Kison said as he looked at their confused faces.

Nakul quickly stepped in front of him and questioned Kison "Okay, so the thing is you were able to beat us down because we are using these primitive weapons or no weapons at all? Do you have any idea of what we have in the ship?" dusting off the dirt over his suit.

"A man's strength doesn't lie in his arms, but the way he uses his arms. Give a man who has courage- a stick to fight with, and he will defeat an army. It's not what he fights with but how he does that matters the most," Kison replied.

Yudhraj walked towards Kison, "Okay, you need to sit down with us and tell us everything. We got the orders from the topmost authority and we were told that the authority owes you."

"Although I wonder, how can the final authority owe anyone anything?" He added.

"Let's take a tour of this place. Let me introduce you to this world and how things are here," Kison said as calmly as he could with a smile on his face and turned towards the dwellings.

Yudhraj whispered to Arjun, "I don't know if we should trust this guy."

Arjun looked at him and said, "We don't have an option here. You know who has asked us to do this job. However, I still don't know why we were asked to carry 'Grade Platinum' weapons with us. This place seems like they don't even have electricity, let alone the infinite energy source."

Everyone followed Kison. He walked towards the ship and stopped abruptly. He was indeed an odd character.

"I think you should probably change your clothes. I am sure you have the outfits with you," Kison said as he looked at the almost invisible ship although Deva doubted it was invisible to him.

Nakul came ahead and with an excited voice said, "Oh! Damn yeah! Can't wait to rock those semi-naked clothes, man! it's messed up at our place. We can't wear such clothes there," and he quickly got into the ship. The other four followed him with much less excitement.

All of them came out wearing traditional Indian clothes. They wore white dhotis just like Kison's, but had their upper body covered with a folded cloth that went across their torso.

"Man! I thought these would be comfortable. How do I walk in these baggy pants?" Nakul said as he tried to walk while holding onto the flare of his Dhoti. It was like looking at a toddler.

Kison smirked at him, "You will be here for a long time, you will get used to this."

None of the others complained about the outfits and everyone was trying to blend in with the surroundings, as it was entirely new for them. Kison started walking and everyone else followed him. They walked a few miles through the jungle until they reached the kingdom.

It was a very different place. Everyone was dressed in traditional clothes. People were traveling on the backs of horses and bullock-carts. People were selling wooden toys, fruits, fresh vegetables, earthen pots, simple things that looked wondrous to them.

"Apples? Are those apples? Nakul was jumping all around the place and he could not believe he was looking at the very symbolic fruit that they had only ever heard about.

Kison looked at Nakul and said, "Yeah, go ahead taste one," and he looked at the stunned fruit-seller who had never experienced such enthusiasm for his wares.

Nakul dashed towards the cart, picked one, and took a big bite, "Delicious…"

Arjun hung his head.

Yudhraj murmured to himself, "Nakul was put in our team so that we could have some stupidity as well."

Bheem said, "Should I bring him back?" as he fidgeted with his Dhoti and was barely even looking at Yudhraj. Which further irritated Yudhraj, as he felt that he was in-charge of a bunch of over-grown kids.

"Never-mind," he said under his breath.

Kison looked at Bheem and cheerfully said, "Its fine! Let him enjoy it. Even you should taste some," although he meant it for Yudhraj.

Meanwhile, Nakul had devoured two apples and had already picked another one. He ate them with so much relish that the juice of fruit was dripping from his face.

Deva left a sigh and said, "Apple! It makes the perfect alcoholic beverage, but that doesn't justify this childish behaviour. Sometimes it feels like it's not me but him who is the youngest of all."

Kison looked at Nakul and said, "Okay, that's it, I'll save him from some embarrassment," and went walking towards him.

Nakul meanwhile finished his third apple and looked at the seller. He was an old guy with wrinkled skin and was shocked to see Nakul's appetite.

"Can I get some more?" Nakul asked the old man.

Kison came from behind, kept his hand on Nakul's shoulder, and said, "I think it's about time we leave."

Nakul looked back at Kison with a mouthful of apple, as he gestured about payment.

The old man's eyes popped out and he froze as he saw Kison in front of him.

Nakul looked at the man and was confused to see what happened.

"Umm, is everything alright?" he asked as he wiped his

mouth with the back of his hand. Some of the apple bits were falling out of his stuffed mouth.

"Yeah, let's leave from here now," Kison said as he pulled him away.

Everyone else observed this from a distance. Yudhraj went near Arjun and whispered, "Did you see that? That's not normal."

Deva got close to Yudhraj and with a very reassuring tone said, "It is fine. I think we are over thinking here. They are from the same neighbourhood, so maybe he didn't take money from him."

Arjun looked at them sheepishly, "It's about time we did what we were supposed to do and not use our brains."

Kison came back with Nakul and joined them.

"Man! Those apples were real. They were real as air! There were seeds in it, the outer skin was real, and it had juice in it which contained sugar. Amazing, right?" Nakul said and smelled like an apple himself.

Everyone ignored him and started walking along with Kison.

People started making way for them as they walked. It felt strange, yet somehow surreal.

Moments later, the people just stood still and looked at Kison who lead the way for the five men. The ordinary people looked as if they were praying.

Arjun calmly observed everything around and said to Yudhraj, "Now, this is strange. This doesn't feel right."

"Very few things about this man feel right," Yudhraj muttered as they followed Kison.

As they walked on, a couple of people joined their hands and bowed their heads in respect when Kison passed them.

"Wow! Now this…" Yudhraj exclaimed to Arjun without looking at him.

They all kept following him until they reached a huge structure. It looked like a fortress but not like the usual one. It wasn't tall, it was spread across the landscape, like a maze. It had walls that were hardly 20 feet tall. Guards stood above them. It looked like it had several compartments, almost a hundred. Right in the middle of the Fortress, there was a pole that hoisted a flag. The flag was huge and had a symbol on it. It looked like the imprints of a bear claw.

Kison took a halt and all the five men stopped too.

He turned back at the men, pointed at the Fortress and said, "This…This is the Fortress of Rule."

"Nothing like a huge fortress," Nakul replied, emphasizing on the word fortress.

He turned towards Nakul and said, "Yes! Not like the usual fortresses, it's not tall, nor on a hill. It's built precisely in the centre of this kingdom."

Arjun kept looking at the Fortress and asked, "What's with dividing it into compartments?"

Kison smirked and said, "It's a long story; let's keep walking. I will tell it to you."

Yudhraj cleared his throat and said, "Hey Kison! We appreciate your hospitality and this tour, but we need answers and we aren't co-operating until you give them to us."

Everyone else seemed to agree.

Kison left a sigh and said, "Not the right time..." before he could finish his sentence, a stone came flying towards him and hit his head hard.

Everyone was shocked.

A humongous man got off a horse and came walking towards Kison. A couple of more people were on horses behind him. He was a bald guy with a dense beard. He looked fierce; the tiger fur around his shoulder added to his personality.

Kison touched his head and found there was blood flowing from where the stone hit him. "Dushan," Kison whispered as he looked at the bald man.

Bheem took a step ahead towards Kison, Arjun quickly stopped him from getting involved.

"Kison, the great Kison! The warrior, the mastermind, the manipulator, and what not, you got guests coming with you?" Dushan said sneeringly as he walked close to Kison.

"Yes!" Kison said as he wiped the blood with his hand.

Dushan looked at Kison and in a very sarcastic tone he said, "Oh, did it hurt? This will hurt more!" and he punched Kison in the stomach.

Kison dropped on his knees and started coughing.

"Men!" Dushan exclaimed at his soldiers, and they all came running towards Kison and started hitting him one by one. They kicked and punched him.

The five from the ship stood watching the scene in shock and confusion.

Yudhraj whispered to Arjun, "This gets weird after every second."

After a while everyone stopped, Dushan looked at Kison who looked like a hundred horses had trampled him.

Dushan said, "You deserve this, you might have won the trust of others, but I am not as blind as my father. I see through your game, and I know one day you will betray us."

Kison got up with a lot of struggle and said, "He might be blind, but you can't even see what's in front of you now," and he scoffed.

Dushan ignored what he said and walked towards the fortress.

Kison looked back at the five men.

Yudhraj hesitated to speak looking at Kison's current condition, "We are going to the ship now, and we want to know the entire story or else we are going back."

"Alright," Kison said in a soft tone.

They walked back where the ship was. Kison sat on a nearby rock, and everyone looked back at him.

"You alright, buddy?" Nakul asked.

"I apologize, I should have told you everything earlier itself," Kison said as he pressed his palm against his swollen chin.

Yudhraj looked at him and said, "This is pretty strange, you effortlessly beat us down, but you get bashed by some normal soldiers? We need to know who you are and what this is about. We want to help you, but you have to tell us everything."

Kison looked up to him and said, "You can achieve things before time but what's not on time is never valued, be it early or late. Now is not the right time, but I can tell you whatever you are meant to know."

Yudhraj looked back at him and said, "Sure, we are listening."

Chapter 4

The 100 Children

K ison wearily sat down on a rock and looked towards the five men.

"This kingdom, it is called 'Yugprasth,' meaning something that is famous across the globe," Kison said as he stopped massaging his chin.

Arjun stared at him sharply, "Keep talking, we are listening."

Kison continued, "I don't know if in your world there is any good vs. bad or such a thing as evil, but I would like to start from there. This place is ruled by the Karvas- The family that has 100 princes. The name of the emperor is King Duta, he is blind..." before Kison could finish, Nakul interrupted by saying, "I think that baldy mentioned this blind guy, but how can a blind guy be a King?" he asked as he scratched his head.

Kison replied, "Yes! He is blind, but he is the King because his father was one. He is the namesake King. His half-brother Vidurm handles everything from behind the throne."

Yudhraj looked confused as he asked Kison, "So why didn't Vidurm become the King? He is anyway handling the kingdom, so why not be King instead?"

Kison smiled and looked at Yudhraj and said, "Everything I am going to say now has a long story; you will have tons of questions, but please be patient. The answers to these questions are not understandable to you right now."

"Okay, continue," Yudhraj whispered.

"Do not underestimate him because of his blindness. He is a competent human being, but less than his brother and yet fate had a different plan for Vidurm- his skin colour is red...." and once again he was interrupted by Nakul.

"Red? Are you serious? Like the colour? What's going on here? He is red, you are blue..." and he abruptly paused as he remembered that he was not supposed to ask questions.

Kison smiled at him and continued, "No one married Vidurm for the same reason, but he never let that affect his administration or his love for his brother. Vidurm doesn't have a great physique, but his mind is sharp as a knife. He knows to use weapons efficiently, but believes that the war can be won by using the strongest muscle of the body- the brain. So that's Vidurm for you."

"Who would marry a blind man?" Nakul whispered almost to himself.

"Good question. But aren't we all blind in our own ways, some can't see what's lying in front of them while some can't see anything at all," Kison replied.

Arjun was shocked to see that Kison grasped what Nakul said even when nobody else could hear him. Doubts rose in his mind as it was the second time Kison heard someone whisper under their breath.

Kison ignored Arjun and continued "King Duta has a wife, and her name is Gundhi- she is no ordinary woman. She is smart; she is strong and knows all the combats and usage of weapons. Want to know something even more shocking? " Kison asked.

Everyone nodded with rapt attention.

"As her husband is blind she decided to blindfold herself for the rest of her life too," Kison replied.

Everyone was shocked to hear this.

Kison continued, "It has been 44 years since their marriage, and she is still the way she was on the second day of her marriage."

Deva broke his silence and said, "That's magnificent. She won't lose her eyesight, but the day she decides to see will be something no one can look away from."

Kison looked at Deva and said, "You are the smartest, and you are the only one who is figuring out everything. You have probably figured out everything so far, haven't you?"

"You know quite a bit about us; please continue. We want to hear why we are here!" Deva said shyly.

Kison smiled as if he knew that Deva would say this and he continued, "Now, King Duta and Gundhi have hundred sons, before you ask me how, let me tell you the story," and he looked at Nakul.

Everyone was curious to understand this weird story that had bought them here.

"It is said that King Duta and Gundhi couldn't conceive a child for a long time, years passed by, yet there was nothing. That's when King Duta decided to seek help from the kul-guru, sage Vyaan (Family priest) to do something about the impossible. The Sage called an Aghori who lived outside the kingdom. People say that he is there since the beginning of the time and will be there till the end of it," Kison said and stopped to regain his breath.

"Fascinating!" Deva whispered again.

Kison continued, "Almost everyone who knew astrology warned King Duta to not go ahead with the plan that he chalked out, but he didn't listen to anyone. He could not let the throne pass outside his blood-line.

"That night he asked the Aghori to perform the ritual; he stood in his huge balcony. He couldn't see but he felt everything. That night the wind didn't blow, the wolves howled the loudest, the crickets were silent and there were no stars in the sky. Even the moon was hiding. The unnatural chill in the air blew through the kingdom. Even the children knew something was deeply wrong."

Kison noticed that everyone sat on the ground and were totally engrossed in the story, he almost smiled and continued, "It wasn't like King Duta was not aware of the consequences but he was blind in many ways. Queen Gundhi was a strong woman. She knew something was going to happen that might change everything forever, but it looked like she was much more willing to do this than anyone else. A woman who makes sacrifices is the strongest of all. Nothing can stop her. Nothing can break her. King Duta was a little scared, but a King is not allowed to show his emotions, especially fear."

"The time for the rituals arrived, the strange Aghori was in the palace. Strong winds blew as he stepped inside the gates, plunging the entire place into darkness."

Everyone was sitting on the grass and listening to Kison when Nakul suddenly questioned: "Oh, this is pretty dramatic, did this really happen?"

Kison nodded his head and got back to the story.

"The guards immediately lit a few lamps. They couldn't light all of them, but there was sufficient light in the palace to guide the way to the Queen's room. Every maid in the palace hid as they saw the Aghori walk in with the Sage.

The Aghori was tall; his entire body was covered with what looked like ashes. He had drooping shoulders and his eyes were dull, yet they looked like they knew a million secrets. He wore nothing but a small saffron cloth around his waist. He had long dreadlocks which were tied in a bun, had a very long beard and he was very skinny. The strange part was that his body had several scars. He had long and unmaintained nails. He carried a small side bag made out of hemp; it looked like a lot of things were stuffed in the bag. He entered the Queen's room; there was a small place for the yagya to be performed. He didn't pay attention to the King or the Queen. He sat near the woods kept in the yagya and burnt them. He then opened his bag and pulled out a few things, they looked like liquid, ashes, and small pieces that looked like flesh. The King and Queen stood silently as they could not see what the Aghori was doing.

Kison stopped again and saw that Sun was about to set, he looked at everyone and said, "I think we should stop here for today, it's been long since I have been talking. We should rest."

Yudhraj got up and blocked Kison's way even before he could move, "We are not done yet. Can we skip to the point where you tell us why are we called here?" Yudhraj questioned in a very firm voice as he stood inches away from Kison.

Kison didn't move but cleared his throat, "Okay if you want to hear more, then allow me to continue," he said.

"The Sage looked at King Duta and the Queen and asked them, "This is the last chance to withdraw. Are you sure you want to do this?"

King Duta replied, "Sage Vyaan, We are pretty sure of what we are doing. This is not just for us but also for the future of Yugprasth…Continue," he commanded the Aghori."

Deva interrupted Kison and asked, "Who was this sage Vyaan guy anyway?"

Kison looked at him and said "Sage Vyaan was not an ordinary sage, he is a great visionary. He left his parents at the age of six to meditate in the forest. People say he achieved enlightenment through meditation and that his soul has been to heaven and is blessed by gods. This is the reason why he stays in the royal palace. He is a great advisor to the King."

Deva tried to comprehend whatever Kison was saying.

Kison got back to narrating what happened that night.

"The Aghori whispered a few Mantras and burnt the woods and began the yagya. He kept on pouring the things that he carried with him.

Usually, the flames burn bright yellow, but there was nothing normal about this fire. This flame was dark red and the flames were uncontrolled as if chained demons wanted to break free. After a lot of mantra chanting, the fire settled a bit. The Aghori put his hand in the burning yagya and cupped a little flame in his hand and dashed hurriedly towards the Queen who was standing at the corner of the room. Her room was pretty huge, so he had to pace towards her. The Queen was terrified as the Aghori stood just a few inches away from her. She couldn't see him but he was so close that she could smell the ash on his body. He had the burning flame in his right hand. He grabbed the Queen's mouth with his left hand, the Queen screamed, and as soon as she opened her mouth, the Aghori stuffed the flame inside and covered her mouth. Her screamed echoed in the entire palace.

Hearing this, Vidurm kicked open the door and ran into the room. He saw the Aghori near the Queen; it took him a few moments to understand what was happening. He didn't give it much thought and pulled his sword out and went running towards the Aghori. King Duta had no idea what was happening, yet he pulled his sword out. Vidurm almost reached near the Aghori and swung his sword to behead him; suddenly, Sage Vyaan yelled out, 'Stop! Don't do it, King Vidurm. Let him do whatever he is doing'. Unaffected by the things that were happening around, the Aghori held the Queen's mouth, tightly.

Vidurm was terrified; he looked at Sage Vyaan in distress.

"What is happening?" King Duta asked frantically.

Queen's mouth was muffled by the Aghori's hands, and she started panicking. The Aghori who looked weak had surprising strength as he held the Queen. "Gulp!" he exclaimed out loud to the Queen, in a rather commanding tone.

The Queen finally stopped panicking and fell on the ground, she wasn't hurt, but she was scared, very scared. She didn't move at all, she wanted to see what happened, but the vow of staying blind stopped her.

Everyone in the room was terrified. King Duta was still unaware of what was happening.

Sage Vyaan walked towards the King and said, "It's all right! It's been done," he said sourly as he looked at the Aghori.

Vidurm stood there, clueless, with the sword in his hand. The Aghori went walking towards the fire, sprinkled a pinch of brown powder in it and the fire went off instantly. The Queen sat on the ground, terrified. Vidurm ran towards the Queen, picked her up, and asked her if she was fine.

The Aghori looked back at all of them and jeeringly said,

"I will come back after 100 days, till then the Queen doesn't step out of this room and eats nothing. She won't be hungry; no one meets her, no one talks to her and see to it that she is not exposed to the sun," and walked away from the room. The entire room was consumed by silence. Sage Vyaan went near them and said, "It's done my King..." with a voice that was covered with regret."

Kison looked around and saw the surprise on everyone's face. The Sun had already set, and it started to get dark. The swifts made noise, yet no one was moving or paying attention to the surrounding. Kison took a deep breath and continued the story.

"Everyone followed what the Aghori said, the Queen was locked in her room, no one went in, nor did she come out. The windows were sealed so that the sun rays don't enter the room.

Those hundred days were the darkest for the entire kingdom, the crops didn't grow well, the kids were sick, the animals behaved strangely, the nights were longer and it was just ominous.

One hundred days were over, and finally, the night had arrived. The Aghori walked into the palace again and stood outside the room. King Duta, Vidurm and Sage Vyaan stood there waiting for him. Aghori stood in front of the door with ashes in his hand and commanded the Sage to open the door.

The Sage gathered all of his courage and opened the lock of the door. As soon as the door opened an utterly pungent smell spread across the palace. It smelt like a dead body was in the process of decomposition. The Aghori threw the ashes towards the room and the smell reduced a bit.

"Wait outside, do not enter unless and until you are asked to," he commanded as he walked into the dark. The room was huge and there was no source of light inside, it looked like a dark cave. The Aghori went inside, and after a while, he lit the oil lamps. Aghori came out covered with sweat, "I need three maids to come and help me," he said, breathing heavily. Vidurm quickly arranged for the maids and asked them to assist the Aghori.

They went inside and saw that the Queen was laying on the bed with her eyes closed and had an inflated stomach."

Kison paused for a second to check the reactions of the men. Everyone was under shock, but he could see the hunger for more in their eyes. It was getting really dark.

Kison continued.

"The Aghori held the Queen's hair with a firm grip, pulled her head up, and poured some liquid in her mouth. A few moments later, her eyes suddenly opened, and she cried out in pain. She held her stomach and kept screaming and groaning. She was in labour. The maids were clueless as this was surprising for them too.

The King who was standing outside was stressed. The screams of the Queen stopped, but he couldn't hear the cry of any baby. King lost his patience and walked inside the room along with Vidurm, as he stepped in, the maids ran out screaming, they looked pale.

"What happened?" the King asked as he heard the screams and could sense the maids running past him.

Vidurm drew out his sword and went inside the room. What he saw shocked him, he froze in fear, he felt as if the land below his feet was slipping and he couldn't understand what he saw. He was losing his grip on reality. He felt chills all over his body. He dropped his sword on the floor. King Duta was even more stressed and tried to understand what was going on.

Vidurm saw what the Queen had delivered and it wasn't a baby, it wasn't even anything close to human. It looked like a huge piece of flesh. It was thick and black in color. It was on the bed and it moved as if it was inhaling and exhaling. Something slimy came out of the cracks on the piece of this flesh.

Sage Vyaan came running inside hearing the thud that was caused due to the falling of the sword on the ground. Sage Vyaan looked at the piece of flesh, and his eyes popped out. "What have I let happen?" he whispered to himself in utter disappointment.

The Queen got up steadily and sat on her royal bed. "What...what happened? wher...where is my child?" she asked, trying to use her voice after so many days. Vidurm and Sage Vyaan looked at each other and had no idea what was to be done next. The silence again consumed the room; they both looked at the piece of the flesh on the bed. It lay there, struggling to move at its place, trying to breathe in air and left out something toxic. The slime that came out of the flesh was burning the cloth of the bed."

The Aghori smiled wickedly and picked up the huge piece of flesh and kept it on the ground. He held the sword that was dropped by Vidurm and mercilessly chopped the piece of flesh. As he chopped a lot of slime squirted out of it resulting in burns on his hand and body but he still didn't stop. His blows were strong and powerful, with each blow the blade dashed on the ground, sparks came out, and the flesh absorbed the sparks.

Vidurm and Vyaan were disgusted to see what the Aghori was doing. He finally stopped. Vyaan looked at the Aghori and saw that he had chopped the flesh into many pieces.

The Aghori halted and he was panting, "Bring 100 vessels and one huge pot filled with water," he commanded Vidurm. Vidurm ran out and asked the servants to bring what was asked for.

Soon the 100 vessels along with the huge pot were kept in the room. The Aghori picked up all the 100 pieces one by one and placed them in the vessels. He got up and dragged the Queen towards the pot. With the same sword, he cut her a little on her left hand. She cried in pain, blood started dripping from her hand as soon as that happened.

He then pushed the Queen away and pulled out a jar from his bag; it had something semi-liquid. He opened the jar and poured the semi-liquid into the huge pot that contained water. It started boiling, and after a while, it stopped. With the same jar, he collected the liquid and poured in all the vessels that had the pieces of flesh in it.

He was done after a while," and Kison stopped.

Everyone was disgusted to hear the story. The stars came out, and the owls started hooting. "Please finish the story," Nakul said with amazement in his eyes yet with the frown of disgust.

"If you say so," Kison replied as he continued to speak.

"The Aghori went walking towards the door, he stopped and looked back. He looked at the King and said in a deep voice, "Greed makes you desire what is not yours, it takes you away from what you truly deserve. I have done what you have asked me to but remember this is not how Humans are born... Jai Shambho," and he left from there.

Everyone in the room was either clueless or disgusted with what had happened. Unaware of this procedure of giving birth."

And Kison stopped again.

Deva's wandering mind had thousands of doubts, but he chose to speak out loud the most obvious, "This is not exactly how it happens at our place, but similar steps are followed when a child is not born. We call it a test tube baby, it is not possible that humans knew about this for centuries and people didn't implement it from the start."

Kison gave half a smile and said, "There are many such things that people from your place aren't aware of, centuries might pass, but some secrets will remain secrets. There are many things you are about to see, things you might have only read in the books or maybe things you might have never even heard of," and he stopped and looked at the peacock that was far from where they were sitting.

It had been Nine months since the night the babies were placed in the vessels. It took exactly nine months for the lifeless pieces of flesh to turn into babies, and they looked almost human. Stronger and bigger than human babies, but they were human.

The storm settled and people accepted the fact that whatever their King did wasn't right and it was going to haunt them. The mistake of one is punishment for all.

The Aghori came back to the palace after nine months when the babies could move and respond to sound and light.

He entered the room where all the children were kept in their cradle. The King, along with Vidurm, was also present in the same room. The babies were crying, and suddenly, when the Aghori entered, they fell silent, and all the babies had a pleasant smile on their faces.

He walked towards the King and said, "You are greedy; this greed is not good. You wished for 100 children and Lord Shiva has given you 100 children but beware, there are things you will have to face because of this," The Aghori said as he stood in front of the King.

"What do you mean?" The King asked.

"Ask Sage Vyaan," the Aghori replied as he moved

away from the King and turned towards the healthiest baby of all.

Vidurm and The King looked at Sage Vyaan, who was standing next to the Queen.

Sage Vyaan came walking towards the King and said, "My King, the way he brought these babies to life is not natural. If the beginning of a thing is not natural, its end will be no different. That's all I understand," and he turned towards the Aghori who held a baby in his hand. He held it in his hands and brought him near the King.

He handed the baby to the King. As the King held the baby in his hand, he realized that the weight of the baby was not normal; he was too heavy for a new-born.

Aghori looked at the King and said "He is the strongest of all, he will be the leader and the next King."

The King couldn't see his child, but he felt the warm blood of the child running through his veins, the skin was soft, the muscles did feel tender, but it had the potential to become rock solid.

"I will name him Diyohan. The strongest of all," The King announced.

Aghori looked at Sage Vyaan and said, "There is something I need to tell you about these babies," and both of them walked towards the corner of the room.

Aghori looked around and whispered to the sage "There are only five babies in the room that are real and rest all of them are clones. The other 95 are just a moving piece of flesh. None of them can be Kings or of a higher authority; however, they are powerful and undefeatable, but they lack the most important part within them."

Sage Vyaan looked scared and fumbled, "The soul?"

Aghori scoffed and said, "They aren't human souls they are something different. The souls of the five main babies are pulled from the deepest corners of hell."

Sage's eyes popped out as he asked, "What have you done?"

Aghori looked back at Vyaan and said, "What? You are the one who asked me to do this! You asked me to go against fate and do this atrocious task. I am merely someone who performed it. Remember this is going to come right back to you someday. If not you, it's going to be the whole world."

Sage Vyaan was terrified to hear the prophecy of the Aghori. He looked at the babies nervously. He was unable to understand what to do next.

He walked towards Vidurm and asked to speak in private. They both went outside the room, and Vyaan told him what the Aghori had warned him about.

"What? This is what he said?" Vidurm asked Sage Vyaan as he was scared too.

"Yes! What should we do? The fate of the whole world lies in front of us. We aren't capable of handling such a huge responsibility," Sage Vyaan said as he saw King Duta playing with one of the babies.

"We have to kill all the babies," Vyaan said in a heavy voice.

"Do you even hear yourself Sage Vyaan? How are you going to do this? And how are you going to convince the King to do so?" Vidurm asked as the colors on his face drained away.

King Duta walked and stood next to them.

"I am aware of the consequences, I know what we have done is unforgivable but that's something I will have to worry about after two decades or so but meanwhile let the kingdom celebrate and let me be happy about the fact that the throne will have someone from the royal family and not someone who doesn't belong to the royal blood."

King Duta turned his back towards Sage Vyaan and Vidurm. He couldn't see his kids, but he could hear and feel more than anyone else could.

Chapter 5

Naming ceremony day

The entire kingdom gathered in the royal court. People whispered things; people knew how the children came to life. They were terrified, yet they plastered their faces with fake smiles because their King had called them to celebrate. The King knew the five babies that the clones were modeled on. Just like a father knows his children.

The first one was named, 'Diyohan.'
The second one was named, 'Dushan.'
The third one, Virakanna.'
The fourth one as, 'Dushalya.'
And the last one as, 'Yutsu.'

They were the future of the kingdom, and it was obvious that Diyohan was going to become the King as he looked like one; he was born with the aura of a King. He was strong even before he could walk, he was smart even before he could understand. He was born to rule, and everyone could see why.

The kingdom celebrated the ceremony with a lot of funfair even though the citizens were half scared to death. The music was in the air, yet the heaviness of fear hung above the kingdom like dark clouds.

That night the King stood in the huge balcony of his palace. Queen Gundhi came walking towards him. She stood next to her husband and asked him, "What are you thinking about? It was a long day. Don't you want to sleep?"

"Not sleepy yet, there are questions in my mind that won't let me sleep," he replied softly.

"What questions my King?" She probed.

The King left a sigh and said, "The things we did to get these children, I hope that doesn't lead to something that is irreversible for mankind. Sage Vyaan suggested we should kill them before they realize their powers and what they are capable of…"

He was interrupted by the Queen who had turned red and spoke in a high pitch "Are you out of your mind? It took us so many years and still we couldn't conceive a baby. Just because the sage says something, are you going to listen to him? You are the King and you decide things. These are our children, and we will raise them to be the best warriors and Kings of the future."

"I am blind, but you aren't, this is selective blindness Gundhi. You are turning a blind eye towards the fact that this involves a bigger risk and we aren't ready to take one right now."

The Queen had lost her patience by now. She wanted to be a mother, and when she finally became one, her husband spoke of killing her babies. It made her furious. "So what? I don't really care what the future has got for us, but for me right now my children are the most important thing in the world. I have given birth to them and I will decide what is to be done with them. I have made sacrifices for this family, not just a life of blindness but also locking myself in that miserable room for 100 days. One hundred days of being alone, not speaking to anyone, not uttering a word, crying to the emotionless walls and 100 days of not knowing what is happening to my body."

The King could not see her face, yet he knew not to push her further. So he kept quiet even though he was feeling what the rest of the kingdom knew already.

Years later...

The royal court was filled with people. The King, Queen Gundhi, Vidurm, Sage Vyaan, Dushan, Virakanna, Dushalya, and Yutsu were holding court. The other clone-sons were somewhere in the palace guarding the royal family.

One of the guards came running into the royal court; he had wounds all over his body. They looked like he was attacked by an animal, he was covered with his own blood and his uniform was shredded in places.

Vidurm, who was sitting next to the King, quickly got up and questioned, "What happened? These wounds, who did this to you?"

He stood before them and said breathlessly, "My King, I

was with prince Diyohan. He wanted to hunt. We went deep into the woods, and we lost our way when a tiger attacked us..."

As soon as the King heard this, he got up from his throne and screamed, "What? Is he fine? Why are you here instead of protecting him?"

Vidurm immediately walked towards the guard, "Forget it! Take me there now."

The guard stammered and said, "I thought that the man-eater tiger was going to attack me, when Prince Diyohan saw this and jumped right in front of the tiger. He started wrestling the beast with his bare hands. I was scared, so I ran away."

The King was shaking with fury as he yelled at the cowardly guard, "How can you even leave him like this. Go with Vidurm right now and help him! GO!" and collapsed on his throne.

Vidurm and the guard rushed towards the jungle.

Yustu, who was sitting next to his mother, leaned in to ask her, "What is it, mother? Aren't you worried for brother Diyohan?'

Queen scoffed and said, "I am worried for the tiger. Your brother is stronger than any man alive. By the time Uncle Vidurm and the guards will reach them; your brother will have torn the tiger into pieces."

Yutsu was surprised to see his mother's confidence.

Yutsu wasn't the warrior kind; he believed that violence

wasn't necessary and things can be handled differently. He also believed that being just and kind is the way to rule. He wasn't like his brothers, he was different even when he learnt the same things his brothers were taught. He was an excellent swordsman.

In the forest...

The guard rode the chariot while Vidurm was sitting behind. He kept his bow and arrow ready.

"We are almost there," the guard said while belting the horses.

Suddenly they heard a huge roar from somewhere in the west. The guard immediately turned the chariot towards the commotion. Vidurm clutched the nock of the arrow and pulled it with a string. He aimed towards the direction they were headed in.

The chariot stopped and Vidurm didn't fire the arrow; instead, he pulled the arrow away from the bow. He stared ahead in shock and fearful awe.

Diyohan sat on a nearby rock, as the tiger fell lifeless in front of him. He had torn the jaw of the tiger by pulling it apart. The tiger was stabbed at many places and he had pierced his entire sword in its back.

Diyohan was panting as he looked at his uncle. Diyohan was now a young man, who was not only powerful but also ruthless. He was of wheatish complexion; he was tall and had an extremely muscular body. He had long hair that he kept open, half of his face was not visible due to his long messy hair and the other half was covered in the tiger's blood. Rather his entire body was covered with the blood.

Vidurm jumped out of the chariot and went running towards Diyohan.

"Are you okay?" He asked his nephew.

"What can happen to me?" Diyohan said with a sense of narcissistic pride.

"Let's go now! Your father is worried about you," Vidurm said as he turned towards the chariot. Vidurm sat inside the chariot but before he could settle down, Diyohan pulled Vidurm's sword and stabbed the guard who was riding the chariot.

"This was for leaving me alone to fight this tiger," Diyohan said as he twisted the sword deep in the guard's stomach.

Vidurm was taken aback to see his nephew behaving like that, but he didn't say anything.

The guard died within a few moments. Diyohan pulled back the sword and pushed the dead guard aside and the dead body fell on the ground with a thud.

He put the sword in his scabbard and sat in the rider's chair and rode the chariot.

They reached the royal court. Vidurm and Diyohan walked inside.

Everyone was shocked to see the blood covered Diyohan.

Vidurm said, "My King, we are back. The prince is safe."

King walked towards Diyohan and said, "My son! Please don't do this again!" and he held him by his shoulders unable to see him covered in blood. As soon as the King hugged him, he felt the sticky warmth of the blood.

Dushan and Virakanna came walking towards them. Dushan looked at him and said, "Brother! It seems like you literally tore the tiger apart," and laughed hard with hands on his stomach.

Virakanna looked around and asked him, "But brother, where is the guard?"

The King too asked him the same question, to which Diyohan replied, "I was fighting the tiger when uncle Vidurm reached there. The guard didn't think for a moment and just came running towards the tiger. He fought bravely, but he died. If it wasn't for him, I wouldn't be alive today," he said in a solemn voice.

Everyone was silent in the courtroom; the Queen had a smirk on her face while Yutsu who was seated beside her, looked curiously at his mother and said "Mother, this is not what you predicted."

"I know my son better than anyone. But yes, if he says this is what happened then let's believe it," she said and giggled. She knew what had happened, but she decided to speak nothing. Although, she looked self-satisfied.

Diyohan was the commander of the entire army; they didn't need an external army as the brothers were sufficient to fight a war. Diyohan was an all-rounder and he led the entire army. The prophecy of him being the almighty was true. He was a ruthless warrior who did not know the meaning of defeat.

Dushan was the one who looked after the fitness of the army. He was bald and was blessed with broad shoulders. A body that was always combat ready; the tilak on his forehead made him almost regal. His dense beard gave him a fierce look. He gave more importance to his fitness than anything else. He spent hours and hours in training for combat. He could stop an elephant with his bare hands. He killed a tiger when he was just 16 years old. Since then, he wore the tiger's fur around his body as a mark of pride.

Virakanna was the one who wielded and designed weapons that could kill anyone and anything. He always carried three swords with him and they all weighed more than five kgs. He made different kinds of swords, used mechanism that was never used before; like pipes that fired multiple arrows at a time, automatic ground weapons that could be placed in the war zone, armours for the animals that served the army and many more such things. He was blind from one eye as he hurt himself while trying to make a weapon that could fire arrows straight into a person's eyes while in combat. It was a weapon that shot out arrows straight at the height of a man's head, something that could directly kill and not leave a chance for recovery.

Dushalya was a motivator, he motivated the entire army when needed, trained them to be as hard as a rock and to be the best. He, along with his brothers, was emotionally strong enough to ruthlessly kill someone and not break a sweat. Dushalya excelled the art of oratory, he could manipulate anyone to do something they never wished to. Just like his other brothers, he was physically fit and had appealing looks. He had a graceful moustache that he twisted often. A Sharp nose and perfect jawline. He wasn't as tall as his brothers, but he was perfect in his own ways. He had long hair that fell to his shoulders. He could live without food and water for days. It is said that he once ate mercury by mistake and still survived.

Yutsu was a very emphatic person. He looked after the people of the kingdom and he was more into administration than war. He wanted peace and he believed in equality, but he couldn't let anything happen to his brothers. He was the chief of the advisors for their army and had a contingency plan for everything. He grew-up but did not grow old. He stopped aging and looked like a boy in his early 20s, A young boy with clean shaved bare face and shiny beautiful hair.

The five brothers stood in front of the King and were ready to take on anything head to head to save the kingdom. The King was proud of them. They all were young and smart, almost ready to rule the kingdom.

Almost".

Chapter 6

The Perfect Warrior

Kison looked at the moon, realizing how late it was. He was exhausted, but the others looked at him with intrigue. "It's too late now, I must leave," Kison said as he got up and stretched his body that was stiff from sitting on a rock for so many hours.

Yudhraj too looked visibly tired, he yawned and stretched his body as he responded to Kison.

"We will talk tomorrow morning; for now you have given us enough to think about."

"There are many things yet to be told. I will see you in the morning," Kison said as he turned towards the jungle.

Nakul looked at him walking towards the woods and asked Yudhraj, "It's so dark, how would he find his way? Should I go with him?"

Yudhraj looked at Kison disappearing in the woods and said, "No, I think he can manage, he seems to know this entire kingdom like his house, but there is something quite strange about him."

Arjun turned towards the Ship's door and touched a rectangular plate which looked like a biometric or fingerprint scanner. As soon as he placed his hand over it, the machine beeped. He moved his hand away, and the machine said, "Identity confirmed. Commander Arjun, Badge Number 15071995. Squad - Heroes of Wars."

The door opened and a ramp slid out of the entrance of the Ship and made way for Arjun to enter. He calmly walked inside the ship and looked over his shoulder at his teammates and found that everyone was looking at Kison disappearing into the woods. He didn't think much of it.

At a point, Arjun was one of the most regarded students from the F.A.T.E. Academy. He was good at everything, be it combat or planning a strategy. Every mission leader asked Arjun to accompany them for the perfect execution. Arjun became a part of the academy quite late, but he caught up well. It seemed like he was born to be the warrior. Things that took years for other students, Arjun learned it within days.

Arjun was very mysterious; his tragic past might have something to do with it. He spoke rarely and only spoke when required. He was one of the very few people from his world that had the knowledge of Archery. Out of numerous lethal weapons, Arjun decided to stick to his bow and arrow. Arjun could turn anything into a weapon if required. His aim was perfect, his every punch was perfect and his every move was well-calculated for perfection. He was the- "Perfect Warrior."

Arjun was trained by the two best teachers from his

world, Dronaji and Bhishmaji. The entire Squad - H.O.W. was trained by them, but Arjun was paid the most attention by his teachers and had special training sessions with them. He wanted the list to begin with his name when it came to the best warriors of all times. Dronaji was responsible for giving him lessons that made him mentally strong, Dronaji believed that a strong body could win you a battle, but a strong mind can win you wars.

Bhishmaji took up the responsibility to teach him the art of weaponry. Under the guidance of Bhishmaji, he learned to use every weapon that ever existed.

Arjun couldn't settle for anything; every day he wanted to be better than what he was yesterday, he knew of no limits. He could not be stopped. But the hunger for being the best made him the most insecure man in the world too. His focus got divided, he was distracted in keeping a watch over people who were getting to his level, of course very few did reach that benchmark but whoever did, Arjun would do his best to beat them. Arjun fought about hundreds of wars over his lifespan. Each time he stepped into the battle, the enemy knew it's going to rain arrows on them. Arjun was undoubtedly the best, but he knew that the other four are unbeatable. He knew that nobody could defeat them, at least not when all of them are together, so the man who never settled for anything settled for just one thing, to be part of this team and that decision made a huge impact on the entire world. The world got a squad of invincible warriors called, 'Heroes of Wars'.

He had quite a reputation in the academy until one fateful day, the day when the pillars of the academy shook. One fine day, everyone got to know that Bhishmaji and Dronaji had gone missing, to his surprise the academy did not carry out any search operation. The case was closed. Arjun knew something was wrong, he started digging into things on his own, finding evidence, searching for proofs. He was aware that the F.A.T.E. did get their major funding from the corporate giants, but he believed that they had nothing to do with his mentors going missing. He knew the system was flawed, but the only reason why he was part of F.A.T.E. was because of his teachers. The fact that his teachers were not there anymore became his reason to part with F.A.T.E. He gave up his commander badge and got into the world to find his mentors on his own.

As a commanding officer of F.A.T.E. Army, he had ruined lives of several intergalactic criminals, who now had him in their world all alone. Cutting ties with the F.A.T.E. not only put him in the list of fugitives but also left him vulnerable. Even so, he wasn't afraid. As years passed, Arjun turned into a bounty hunter; his need for survival took him to dark places. The darkness was not just on the outside but now in the inside too. However, he had his personal rules of never hurting children or mothers. His tough life made him ruthless!

IN THE SHIP

The Ship's door was left open as he walked through its hallway. The Ship had fine L.E.D. lights across the hallway to guide the person walking. It was dark. He reached the Assembly Hall which was basically the cockpit too. The

Assembly hall had a huge circular table that projected holographic images. It displayed some infographics that included the time, date, location, surveillance footage of everything happening within 1 km radius. The Assembly hall was linked to the eight different paths that lead to the other chambers.

Arjun went up to the holographic table, and as soon as he was near it, he was greeted by a robotic voice.

"Hello Arjun, how can I help you today? How was the city tour? You took more time than estimated."

"Yes. Thanks for asking. We had some work."

"Very well, is there anything you need from me?" the voice asked.

"Yes, Archisa, please show me the surveillance footage of the last 10 minutes."

Archisa was the name of the A.I. of the ship. She was named Archisa by Yudhraj, as it meant the 'ray of light.' They had been through the darkest places in the universe, and the ship had provided them with utmost assistance. She was programmed to help them with everything they needed from an A.I. Though she was programmed, she understood the men very well.

"Here they are," Archisa said and the holographic images were projected in front of him. It displayed many footages running at the same time

Arjun kept scanning the surveillance footages, looking for something he could not find. He heard the footsteps of his teammates approaching the ship, and he quickly pressed a button and the footage was gone.

He could hear Nakul's voice fading in.

"Man! I am very hungry but I think we had a lot for today. How greatly entertaining these stories were, right Deva?"

"I am trying to understand a few things happening here, especially the climate. It is affecting our body in a way that we can notice," Deva said, ignoring Nakul's stupid questions.

Yudhraj looked at Deva with agreement while he shared his observation, "I think just like other planets, we might take some time to adapt here, but this feels very much familiar to what it feels like at home. Except for the fact that this place feels rich," and he looked at his hands.

Bheem touched his arms and said, "Yes, this makes sense."

Bheem had a muscular body, and it seemed that hardly anything could penetrate that thick skin. He spent the entire day working out or either munching on something.

Arjun walked towards the hallway that led to his chamber; he stopped at the entrance of the hallway and looked at his comrades.

"Team! I think we should sleep. Let's wait for Kison to come here tomorrow and let's ask him a few more questions," and he retired to his room.

Bheem went towards the pantry and opened some packed food and started hogging. Everyone was soon in their own chambers.

Arjun entered his chamber and the door automatically closed. He went near the wall and it automatically opened from the centre. It was his personal arsenal; there were many arrowheads and shafts. Along with numerous amount of guns and grenades. He placed his bow at the corner of the arsenal and mounted his quiver on the wall.

He turned his back towards the arsenal and the door closed. He went walking towards a huge cylindrical shaped object that was lying horizontally on the ground with a lot of wires connected to its sides. It looked like a sleeping pod. It had a small rectangle glass at the top.

He tapped the badge on his chest and the text read-'Sleep-Mode'. Many tiny particles came out of the badge and covered the clothes he wore. Within a few seconds, it formed a body-hugging suit, yet it seemed very comfortable, and it looked stretchable. The lid of the sleeping pod opened and Arjun lay on the comfortable bed which was inside.

The pod closed. There were white lights inside the pod and the glass was right in front of his face. Arjun tapped a button which was near his finger and Archisa spoke, "Hello Arjun, what time would you like to get up tomorrow?"

"5:00," He replied.

"Noted, do you want the emergency alarm to go off if something goes wrong? Or you want strict D.N.D. action?" She inquired.

Arjun took only a second and said, "No! Let the alarms go off and wake me up."

"Alright! Commander Arjun."

"Don't call me that, I am not the commander anymore. That's the past, and it's gone, just like the moment that just passed away. If it's bad, forget it; if it's good, relive it. In this case, I would like to forget it."

"For me, you shall always be the most important part of the organization," she replied in a rather pleasant voice.

"Goodnight, Archisa," Arjun said, ignoring her praises and decided to sleep.

An invincible warrior who turned into a criminal, Arjun had a story one could only imagine in their dreams.

Chapter 7

Empathy, Courage, and Strength

The next morning.

Alarms went off in the ship.

Arjun woke up with a start and the lid of his sleeping pod popped open. He raised both his legs in the air and jumped out of the pod. He rushed towards the arsenal and picked up his bow and quiver. He tapped his badge and it read 'Outdoor.' The particles covered his body and turned into a black body-hugging suit. He went running towards the assembly hall. Bheem, Yudhraj and Deva quickly joined him.

"What happened?" Bheem asked Archisa!

"It's a distress call from Nakul," Archisa quickly replied.

Yudhraj grimly looked at the screen and said, "Connect us to his coms, right now."

"He left his coms in the ship, but I have sent his location on your badge," and the holographic image of the map popped out in front of everyone.

"Let's go!" Yudhraj exclaimed as he briskly walked towards the exit door.

Everyone hurried towards the location which was displayed in the holographic map. Though Arjun was the one with perfect physique, Yudhraj ran just next to him. Arjun looked at him from the corner of his eye. This didn't give rise to his competitive feelings; he knew what gave Yudhraj the strength to run faster than the perfect warrior. He ran behind Yudhraj and was followed by Bheem and Deva. Yudhraj drove his energy from his emotions. He was not as proficient as Arjun, but he had enough strength to fight against an army and not break a sweat.

Yudhraj was a just and honest ruler. He was not only the ruler but a friend to every person living there, a son, a brother and a watchful guardian. His position never gave him a sense of pride; instead, it made him feel more responsible for the betterment of society. Yudhraj topped the Community Administration Program in F.A.T.E and opted to look into the peaceful governance of the people. Yudhraj was second to none, and nobody understood people like he did.

In his young age, Yudhraj lived on the streets with few other boys. As the orphanage he belonged to was destroyed, he had nowhere else to go. Yudhraj could have easily gone into any other orphanage, but he realized that there are other children along with him and he felt that it was his responsibility to look after them, voluntarily. Every day he looked at the cadets of F.A.T.E marching out for daily drills and wished to join the organization someday. He hustled daily to keep the others happy and alive.

One day Bhishmaji stepped out of the academy campus and decided to see what's going on with the local people. He hovered on his bike and saw that a young boy, 11 or

12 years old, was being chased by a group of men. He decided not to get involved but quietly spectate. He was impressed to see how the little boy dodged six full grown men; he apparently stole some food from a restaurant and was running away. The kid blindly entered an alley, but he was out of breath and had to slow down. As he did, one of the men finally caught hold of the little boy; grabbed him by his collar and nailed him against the wall. The little boy held the packet of food tightly. He wasn't strong, nor did he have a healthy body. If someone punched him, he probably wouldn't even get up for a day. His bones were visible and he wore ragged clothes.

"You bloody thief!" One of the men exclaimed.

The little boy struggled hard to run away, but he was surrounded by the men.

Bhishmaji didn't interfere yet. He kept on looking at the scene from the top a building.

"Let me go!" The little boy exclaimed.

"You know we can hand you over to the authority for theft and you are never getting out," Another man said as he rolled his sleeves and stood in front of him.

"No! Let me go!" he exclaimed though he wasn't in a position to be demanding,

The man who held him by his collar said, "I don't believe in the law, I would rather take it in my hand and serve justice," and slammed the little boy on the wall.

One of them slapped him with force; the blow was strong enough for the kid to make him cry. The man who was holding him threw him on the ground, and everyone took turns to kick the little boy. Bhishmaji still didn't intervene. He saw that the little boy gripped the packet even harder. Someone pulled out a laser saber from his back pocket and lit it up.

Bhishmaji had seen enough, he jumped from the top of the building to the wall of another one that was very close to it and back to the first building's wall closer to the ground and landed on the floor.

"Enough! Gentlemen," Bhishmaji said in a calm yet deep voice.

Everyone looked back as the voice echoed in the alley, Bhishmaji stood in front of them. He looked like he was in his late thirties and had an exceptionally fit body.

A perfectly groomed salt and pepper beard and hair. The slight wrinkles on his forehead didn't take his charm away, nor did the scar on his right cheek. He wore a white coloured skin suit which had padding at various places; he wore an overcoat just so that people don't see his uniform. The skinsuit which he wore was the uniform of F.A.T.E. The black suit was for the warriors and the white suit for the heads of the academy.

"Leave the kid alone, now!" Bhishmaji commanded as he walked towards the men.

"Stay out of this! This is none of your business. He stole from us," The man who slapped the little boy said.

"It's okay, He is just a kid and he made a mistake. Let him go," Bhishmaji said as he looked at the boy struggling to get up.

One of them came near Bhishmaji, looked him in the eye and said, "I think it's your time to leave, we will take care of this."

Bhishmaji didn't move.

The man went near the boy and slapped him again.

Looking at this, Bhishmaji instantly paced towards the men, he jumped in the air and side kicked one of the men. The man fell miles away. Bhishmaji landed on his legs and looked at the other men

"Let's make this a fair fight, shall we gentlemen?" Bhishmaji said as he was ready to take them on.

Three of the men looked at each other and went running towards Bhishmaji.

"Apologies for the 'to-be-broken bones!'" Bhishmaji whispered as he nodded his head.

One of them swang his hand and threw a punch at Bhishmaji with force. Bhishmaji swiftly ducked and moved sideways below him and punched him with an uppercut. The punch landed on the man's chin and it hurt him pretty bad. Bhishmaji quickly got up and noticed that another man barged towards him with a laser saber in his hand, the man swung his hand in the air, moving his saber towards Bhishmaji. Bhishmaji blocked his hand effortlessly by holding his forearm and twisted his wrist making the saber drop on the ground. Bhishmaji twisted his wrist more and turned him around, folded the man's hand behind his back and kicked him in his knee pit. The man yelled in pain and fell on his face.

Bhishmaji charged towards the other two men. With the momentum, he punched another man. He was quick in his movements and punched the last man with his left hand by going one step ahead.

Everyone was on the ground now, grunting and coughing. He looked around and saw that the boy had fled away. Even after fighting five men single handed, Bhishmaji was not even huffing. He went towards the other side of the alley and saw the boy running across the street. Bhishmaji followed him.

A while later the boy reached an old woman, she was weak and leaning against a huge dustbin.

"Here! This is for you, have some food,"the little boy said as he stood in front of the lady.

Few other boys came and sat beside the old lady, there wasn't enough food, but he managed to split it amongst everyone except for himself.

"What about you?" one of the boys asked.

"Ah, I ate a lot today. Brought some for you. Have fun," the little boy said as he left from there.

He went walking towards the end of the alley and stopped abruptly; there was a loud grumbling voice in his stomach. He felt weak and dropped to his knees.

"Since how long have you been hungry?" A voice came from behind.

The little boy didn't have the strength to even turn around, he dropped on his back and saw Bhishmaji standing next to him. His eyesight was blurry and he felt weak. The little boy couldn't speak as the weakness was already eating him up.

Bhishmaji bent down and made him sit on the floor.

"Three days," the boy whispered.

"Three days? And you gave all the food to other people?" Bhishmaji asked as he held his little palm.

"Yes! They needed it more than I did. I am the eldest, and it's my responsibility to feed them."

"Why are you being so hard on yourself?" Bhishmaji asked.

"Responsibilities. When you acknowledge them, they give you extra courage," he replied in a soft voice.

"How old are you?" Bhishmaji asked him listening to him talk in such a mature manner.

The little boy couldn't even speak properly, stammering he said, "Ele...Eleven.Eleven years"

Bhishmaji had a slight smile on his face as if he could relate to the misery of this child.

"What's your name, son?"

The little boy had a smile on his face, and with pride, he said, "Yudhraj," and he fell unconscious....

Chapter 8

The Coronation

Yudhraj was galloping and soon the others were quite behind. He reached the place which showed Nakul's location.

He was huffing and looking around to spot Nakul, everyone else was there soon enough, and they just stopped as they saw what was in front of them.

They all saw Nakul playing with a puppy!

"What the hell?" Arjun said, trying to catch his breath.

"Oh here you guys are, look what I found," Nakul said rather playfully as he rubbed the belly of the puppy.

"You just gave the ship a distress call; do you understand what that means?" Arjun exclaimed.

Nakul figured he had messed up, he got up from the ground slowly, embarrassed.

"Ugh! I forgot my coms in the ship and I thought this was the best way to call you guys here," Nakul muttered as he scratched his head.

Bheem from behind said, "Is that the offspring of a 'Canis lupus familiaris?'"

Deva went near the puppy but maintained a safe distance from it; he observed its behaviour for a while. The puppy sat on his two legs and kept looking at Deva with his shiny eyes.

"Yes! He is, it is called a pup! They exist here," Deva said as he saw him calmly sitting on the ground.

Yudhraj walked towards Nakul, looked him in the eye and said, "Be a little responsible Nakul, this is not a joke," Yudhraj was not happy with what Nakul did. Before he could get any more mad at Nakul, he felt something near his toe.

The puppy was licking Yudhraj and wagging his tail. Yudhraj picked the little puppy in his arms and looked at it.

"Be careful, they are very delicate," Deva exclaimed as he saw Yudhraj picking up the puppy. He looked happy as it settled in the strong arms of Yudhraj.

"See? He likes you," Nakul said.

The puppy suddenly looked towards the other side and his ears stood up. Everyone looked towards the direction the puppy looked at. They heard someone approaching them, Yudhraj stepped back as he held the little puppy in his arms.

From behind the bushes, came Kison!

"Oh! It is you!" Nakul said as he heaved a sigh of relief.

"How did you even know we were here?" Arjun asked Kison!

"I saw you running in this direction and I just followed you."

"Also it looks like you made a new friend," Kison said as he walked near Yudhraj.

Deva was curious to know more about the dog; he went near it and asked Kison, "Well! Are they really kind and loving?"

"Yes," replied Kison as he touched the head of the puppy. The puppy instantly calmed down and closed his eyes.

"So are you ready? We have to go to the kingdom of Yugprasth today. Why? I will tell you while we walk towards the kingdom," Kison said as he pointed to the route that lead to the kingdom.

Yudhraj kept the puppy on the ground, he looked at Kison and said, "Sure, Let's move."

Everyone turned the dial of their badge and their suits turned into the standard traditional wear. They were now wearing dhotis and short kurtas. They all followed Kison and started walking away. Yudhraj looked back at the puppy and smiled at him as he wagged his little tail.

"We are going to the Palace. Today is the coronation of the Prince," Kison said as he walked away expecting the others to follow him.

Nakul ran behind him and said, "Damn, that's cool. This world is new for us! I am glad we are getting to be part of this ceremony."

"A big part," Kison corrected him.

"Stop!" Arjun exclaimed.

"Yes?" Kison replied

"What do you mean by a big part? If we have to assassinate someone, you have to tell us now! If we have to attack the Palace, you still got to tell us now! We are fed up of surprises and we want to know the real purpose," Arjun said as he stood in front of Kison.

"Purpose? You will only know your purpose when the right time arrives. Wait for it, Arjun. Wait. You have nothing to know now! Please, relax Arjun. I am just taking you to the ceremony. I don't mind telling you what your mission is, but that's too early for now and I want you guys to adapt to the surroundings first, RELAX!" Kison said as he emphasized on the word relax and slightly touched Arjun's shoulder.

"Also, you should keep your bow and arrow back in the ship," he added. Arjun could not look away from Kison and slowly nodded at his words.

Kison always had this calm tone like everything was under his control and as if he was aware of every consequence that might take place.

"So we are heading towards the Palace now, where the ceremony is taking place. You are going to thoroughly enjoy the ceremony," Kison reassured them.

They walked out of the jungle and entered the kingdom,

the streets were empty, the houses were closed and it was all just vacant.

Deva looked around and asked Kison, "Hey? Where is everyone, if today is the coronation, then everyone should be celebrating, right?"

"Everyone is in the palace; the celebration is taking place over there," he replied.

After walking a few miles, they finally reached the Palace. The entire Palace was decorated with flowers and garlands. It was raining rose petals everywhere. They heard the music of dhols and mridungum from far and it looked like the entire kingdom had descended to the Palace.

"Scammy Kammy! That looks sick!" Nakul exclaimed.

He started walking quickly as he was mesmerized with the beauty of the Palace.

They all stood in front of a huge gate of the Palace that spread across acres; the vast floor was covered with various colourful flower petals. The huge door was open and was covered with garlands. They walked past the open lawn as they continued towards the royal court where the ceremony was set to happen.

It was a huge lawn and at the end, was the entry for the royal court. The lawn was surrounded with gateways that lead to a different part of the fortress, above each gateway, there were two storeys built. It looked like one big structure. The storeys had huge balconies and a couple of guards were stationed over there. A few had spears and others had bow and arrow with them. Each one of them was extremely alert and in a ready to kill position. Arjun observed each of them keenly. His pace reduced as he was engrossed in observing the formation of the guards.

Deva slowed down a bit and walked beside Arjun

"Hey! Is everything alright?" Deva asked as he knew that Arjun is not the kind of guy who would waste his time on something that didn't matter.

"This formation and the way these men are stationed seems very familiar to me. Something I would do if I had to set the security for something so big. The strength of an army is not in the number, but in their positioning. This seems like the work of a specialist," Arjun replied while he was observing the tight security.

"Yes, the security is way too tight, but this is expected. It's the King's Palace and today is their big day. Not like we know a lot about this place, but that's all I understand," Deva said as they walked towards the royal court.

They finally reached the royal court; it was vast and magnificent. All the hundred brothers were present, and rest of all the other members were sitting in the court. There was a magnificent throne at another end of the court. The court was divided into two parts with a huge space that looked like an open ground. The common people gathered on both sides. A huge stairway was connected to both sides of the royal court. Behind the Throne, there were hundred and one Brahmins doing yagya for the success of their future King. On the outside of the court, ox and goats were sacrificed for the wellbeing of the kingdom. On the floor above, there were many guards present who had a complete watch over everyone.

Kison, along with the five, entered the courtroom.

"So, you guys can stand there," Kison pointed towards a place which had an empty chair and walked towards the crowd. That place had seating for the members of the royal court and a barricade divided it from the standing area of the common men.

All of them were clueless about why he specifically asked them to stand there. They all made their way towards the place where Kison had shown them.

"Don't lose yourself in the crowd Nakul!" he said to himself.

They all walked towards the chair and found Kison sitting on the chair.

Everyone was confused to see Kison sitting on the chair meant for the members of the royal court.

Deva left a sigh and said to himself, "I am sure this is going to get even weirder as time passes."

Bheem looked at him and said, "Well, I am prepared."

Suddenly loud trumpets blew and all the musicians started playing louder. The trumpets, the Dhol and the Nagadas echoed in the royal court.

Everyone looked at the grand stairway where they saw The Blind King, the blindfolded Queen and Diyohan walk down towards the Throne. Following him were his four brothers and then the remaining 95 clones joined them.

Diyohan walked between the King and Queen. They reached the middle of the royal court and were welcomed with great applause. The Queen wore a heavy embroidered dress that caught the eye of every lady present there and the King was in his royal suit that had diamonds studded on it. Diyohan too wore the same royal outfit and had a sword on his waist. They walked till the Throne and the Queen sat on the royal chair that was stationed right next to it. The King sat on the Throne and Diyohan was standing next to him. He was all excited for his big day and his happiness knew no bounds. The King was sure about the fact that he will be the next emperor and nobody out there had the courage to fight Diyohan and win against him.

The King raised his right hand in the air and the entire hall fell silent. Everyone was excited for their new King. Sage Vyaan joined them and stood next to Diyohan. He came forward and announced with a voice that was loud and filled with pride, "Today is the day when Yugprasth gets its new King. After five decades of leadership under King Duta, his eldest Son Diyohan will take over the throne and rule the kingdom. He will bring success and prosperity to all of us."

The applause was even louder this time.

The King got up and said, "My people! I have served you each and every day for the last fifty years, gave my blood and sweat for this kingdom. In spite of me being blind, we have managed to build a great kingdom. My blindness has not come in the way of my leadership, but I am sure we could do with more vision for the future. Today my eldest Son, who is the master of all, takes the throne and becomes the King. May I present to you the future of Yugprasth," he then removed the crown off his head and handed it over to Sage Vyaan to coronate Diyohan.

Diyohan sat on the throne, he was visibly delighted.

Before sage Vyaan could coronate him, he looked at the crowd and announced.

"If anyone thinks he/she can be a better leader than Diyohan, they can step forward now. Now is the time to speak up."

Everyone was quiet; no one uttered a word.

Diyohan looked at Vyaan and said, "Sage Vyaan, no one is going to come forward to challenge me. Let's do this already."

He then walked towards Diyohan to coronate him.

"I OBJECT!" A voice echoed in the entire Royal Palace.

It was Kison.

The King was taken aback when he heard Kison's voice.

"Kison! What is wrong? Are you planning to challenge Prince Diyohan?" The King asked instantly.

Deva looked at Arjun and Yudhraj, "Here we go; I knew that Kison was up to something."

Kison got up from his chair and stood in front of the throne. Everyone started whispering amongst themselves. Diyohan was really angry by now, he waited for this day for years and now when he was inches away from achieving it, Kison was going to spoil it.

Sage Vyaan was shocked to see this; he walked a few steps towards Kison. Diyohan saw the crown going a little far from him; he got up from his throne and looked at Kison with rage, his eyes turned red.

Sage Vyaan held the crown in his hand and approached Kison, "what are you doing Kison"? You cannot challenge him. With the powers you have, no man can stand against you, you therefore cannot challenge the throne."

Kison smiled and said, "Right, I cannot..."

And he pointed towards the five men!

"I challenge you on behalf of them, they will fight you, and one of them will be the Ruler of this kingdom," Kison said, and there was utter silence in the royal court.

Chapter 9
Two Pillars

"What the hell…" Yudhraj exclaimed.

Kison's words had them all frozen in place, they stood there shocked as he pointed a finger at them.

"This is going so bad," Nakul thought.

"What is going on?" Diyohan yelled from the other end at Kison who stood in the center of the royal court. Kison didn't look at the five men but kept pointing his finger towards them. The entire court was quiet. Nobody understood what was happening. Nobody said anything; all the other members of the royal court were stunned. After a brief silence, Diyohan who was very angry moved away from his throne and started walking towards Kison. Sage Vyaan immediately stopped him.

"Prince, don't leave the throne unattended. Please calm down. I will deal with them," as he tried to stop Diyohan.

Kison looked at the courtroom, it was filled with people who had no clue and were waiting to know what he had planned. He cleared his throat and looked at King Duta.

"My King! With all due respect, you spoke to me a couple of days ago. You were really worried about your sons, that's when you asked me if I know someone who could defeat Diyohan! The father inside you took over the King that day. You asked me as the royal advisor and I didn't say anything. Here is my open challenge to Prince Diyohan and here are the men who are far more capable than anyone I know."

Dushan glared at the five men and walked towards Kison.

"Who are these people? Some ordinary men? Before anyone challenges my brother he has to go through me," Dushan said looking straight into Kison's eyes.

Deva thought that an intervention was necessary; he made his way between two royal chairs and walked near Kison.

Dushan looked at him and laughed.

"You? You will fight me? Look at yourself. It won't take me even a second to put you down."

Deva looked really tiny in front of the huge Dushan. Deva was smart and he could handle situations very well. But this one was out of his control, and he knew he couldn't stop this, but he could only slow it down till Yudhraj and Arjun planned something.

"It is not like you can put me down in a second but why to fight over something that is…." Before he could finish his sentence, he was punched hard in the face by Dushan. It was so powerful that Deva was thrown a few feet away.

"NO!" Yudhraj exclaimed, and he ran towards Deva.

Arjun quickly turned towards Nakul and Bheem.

"Nakul, rush and see if Yudhraj needs any help! Bheem, Come with me."

Even before Arjun could finish his sentence, Nakul jumped over the chair and went running towards Deva.

Yudhraj was on his knees as he looked at Deva, who was struggling on the ground.

"Let me help you, Deva," Yudhraj offered.

"He punched me so hard, this hurts a lot," he said as blood spluttered from his mouth.

Arjun and Bheem stood in front of Dushan; meanwhile Kison stood near the corner and watched everything. He had a mischievous grin on his face and looked at Diyohan who was mad with rage.

"Now it begins..." Kison whispered

Bheem walked towards Dushan with his fist clenched.

"He was just talking, you shouldn't have done that!"

"Oh, so you are going to fight me? Let me know if you can hit as hard as you look," Dushan said in a sarcastic tone to mock Bheem.

Bheem charged towards him with his fist closed, he jumped towards him and punched him in his chest. The impact was hard; Dushan lost his balance and went a few steps behind.

"Nice punch! But that's all you got?" he asked as he charged towards Bheem.

Meanwhile, Arjun was observing all the guards who had pointed their arrows and spears towards them.

He looked at the combat between Bheem and Dushan.

"There is no way out of this, either fight all of them or surrender," he said to himself.

Suddenly he saw that Diyohan snatched a spear from one of his guards and aimed it towards Bheem. He rushed towards Bheem to catch the spear, Arjun jumped and caught it in mid-air, front flipped and landed on his feet.

He looked at the spear, held it tight in his hand and ran towards Diyohan with great speed. He twirled the spear in front of him and took a long jump towards Diyohan as he pointed the spearhead towards him.

Before he could stab Diyohan, someone jumped from the ceiling in front of Arjun and kicked him while he was still in mid-air; it was so fast that Arjun couldn't see the person jumping down or even when he was kicking him. The kick was firm; it felt to him as if he was getting hit by an elephant. Arjun dropped the spear and fell on the floor. He grunted and tried to get up, the kick made him a little dizzy.His head was spinning for a while, he looked around and saw Yudhraj ignoring everything and trying to pick up Deva who was badly injured. Nakul didn't help Yudhraj, instead he looked at the person who kicked Arjun. Nakul's eyes popped out and his jaw almost touched the floor, he was frozen.

Arjun rigorously shook his head to gain his senses back

and left a sigh in anger; he saw that the spear was lying next to him. He grabbed it and got up quickly even before he could gain his balance. His vision was bit blurry, yet he charged towards the person who kicked him, as he ran a few steps his vision got back to normal and things were clear. What Arjun saw put him in a state of shock, he dropped the spear on the ground, controlled his momentum, and slowed down. Bheem looked at the entire scene and stopped too; Dushan took the opportunity and punched him in his torso.

Arjun stood in front of the man who was far away from him. He was a strong tall man; he seemed like in his early fifties. He had long hair and beard which was of salt and pepper shade and a scar on his right cheek. The armour on his body was heavy and looked like he was ready for a battlefield.

"Master Bhishamji?" He exclaimed in a state of shock.

Yudhraj and Deva turned towards Arjun and saw that Bhishmaji stood in front of Diyohan to protect him.

"This can not be true," Arjun said to himself.

"Dare you lay a finger on our prince," Bhishmaji yelled at Arjun.

"Bhishmaji! What are you doing?"

"How do you know my name?" Bhishmaji asked him as he stood in front of Diyohan.

"It is me, Arjun! Don't you remember me?" and he walked towards Bhishmaji.

"Stop where you are, or else I will be forced to kill you," Bhishmaji exclaimed as he raised his hands towards the archers present on the second storey.

"What are you waiting for? Kill them now," Diyohan commanded.

Suddenly Kison walked in the centre of the court as casually as he could.

"Wait wait wait! Everyone calm down! Bhishmaji cannot kill these men, even if he does, that would mean that the competition was eliminated because the men from Royal family aren't capable of fighting."

Nakul looked at Yudhraj and said, "I can't take this anymore! What is this?"

"I am as clueless as you are Nakul," Yudhraj said as he kept his eyes on Kison.

Bhishmaji walked down the steps of the throne and went near Kison.

"I don't care. These men attacked the royal family. Leave the challenge aside," He said as he ignored Arjun.

The five men were shocked to see someone who looked like their mentor stand in front of them with hate in his eyes.

Deva's eyesight was blurry, but he figured out that whatever is happening is not okay.

"Yudhraj! I think you should get there..." Deva said as he leaned a little towards Nakul.

Yudhraj walked towards Bhishmaji. The distance became longer as he walked, after every step he took towards Bhishmaji, tons of memories crossed his mind, but he didn't lose his composure. He looked at Arjun who was in a state of shock to see his mentor standing in front of him. He was shattered into pieces as he was on his knees staring at Bhishmaji. Arjun didn't know if he should be rejoicing as he had finally found his mentor after looking for him in every corner of the universe or to be devastated with the fact that the man who raised him like a son didn't even recognize him.

"Master Bhishmaji, don't you remember us?" Yudhraj said in a polite yet firm voice.

Diyohan was confused to see what was happening; he had no clue why these people were calling Bhishmaji by his name and asking if he knows them.

"Bhishmaji!" Diyohan exclaimed

He instantly looked behind.

"KILL THEM," Diyohan commanded!

"As you wish, my Prince," and Bhishmaji swung his hand in the air to punch Yudhraj.

"wait!"a scream came from the other end of the court.

Bhishmaji stopped.

A man came walking towards them. He was in his mid-fifties as well, he was bald and had a white beard, features like that of an alpha male, he was wearing a maroon robe which had golden embroidery at the ends.

The way the robe lay over his body, it took the shape of his muscles.

Everyone turned towards the voice.

Yudhraj was the first one to look at him, his eyes popped out and a shiver ran down his spine. He was left startled.

"What the hell again?" Nakul screamed this time.

Arjun, who still couldn't get over the first shock, screamed "Master Dronaji?"

Deva couldn't comprehend what was happening; Dushan's punch had already weakened him. Nakul held him and maintained his balance.

Bheem was shocked too; he somehow managed to walk and stand beside Yudhraj.

"What is happening Yudhraj? This is not possible," Bheem whispered to him.

"I have no idea, but our mentors don't seem like they remember us, I am not even sure if they are our mentors or some alternate reality," Yudhraj whispered back.

The person who looked like Dronaji said, "Bhishmaji, you cannot kill them. Kison has challenged the royal throne on behalf of these men. Killing them will be an act of cowardness; it's fair to give a chance to anyone who challenges the throne.

We have trained the prince in a way that no one can defeat him. If Kison thinks these men can fight the prince, then be it. Let them have combat, but the ultimate end would be death."

Bhishmaji moved a step behind as he heard what Dronaji said and he looked at Diyohan.

Diyohan looked back at him and said, "Why just one? I challenge all of them, the fifth one does't even look like he can stand up for next few days so I'll spare his life," referring to Deva.

Suddenly Kison walked in between and said, "That's unfair! You will be against four of them. That's not an even fight. You choose your opponent."

Arjun who was deep in shock, finally came back to his senses as he heard Kison's words. By now Arjun had enough, everything had piled up to an extent where he couldn't maintain his calm anymore. He experienced several emotions, happiness, sorrow, anger, betrayal, all at once. He looked at Kison with contempt for putting him through this roller-coaster of emotions. Arjun had finally lost his temper.

He rushed towards Kison and held him by his robe. As soon as he did this, there was a huge gasp in the entire hall, including Diyohan.

"Don't!" Kison said calmly as he looked into Arjun eyes with a straight face.

"What are you up to? we have had enough of your games. We are not here to fight someone we don't know or someone who doesn't even know us," Arjun said as he moved a little closer to him, his grip was still firm on Kison's robe.

A murmur spread across the courtroom, Yudhraj could

hear people speaking things in the distance "How can he hold him? This is impossible, God forgive him, oh watch him turn into dust now."

Yudhraj quickly walked towards him and whispered in his ear, "Arjun, don't do anything stupid. This doesn't feel right. People here are murmuring something and we don't want to mess with this guy. He is the one who called us here, relax."

"Yes, relax Arjun," Kison said with a smile on his face.

Kison firmly removed Arjun's hand from his robe, moved aside and looked at Diyohan.

Diyohan who was a little taken aback to see everything. He quickly cleared his throat and said, "I am enough to kill these chickens, but I will give them a fair fight too. My three brothers will join this battle."

"So, It's settled then," Kison said.

Dronaji stepped forward and announced, "Alright! The ceremony is prolonged until the championship gets over. The kingdom will be ruled by King Duta till then. The championship will start the day after the full moon. That is in the next three days."

There was silence in the court; everyone was worried except Kison. He had a smile on his face as he looked at the throne.

Chapter 10

Mission Abort

The men stood in the centre of the hall as everyone looked at them. Some nodded their heads, while some shared a smile.

"I think we should leave," Nakul said as he looked around.

Yudhraj noticed that Bhishmaji and Dronaji were talking to Diyohan; he had the urge to go and speak to them.

Yudhraj looked at Arjun and said, "Let's further discuss this in the ship," as he walked towards the main exit.

Inside the ship

Everyone was standing in the main hall while Deva was in the emergency room. Nakul looked at how badly the punch had affected him. His face was swollen and turned black and blue. Deva was placed inside a pod which looked similar to the sleeping pod. It was filled with a semi-solid liquid and he wore an oxygen mask that kept his breath pattern normal. A small screen mounted on the nearby wall showed a diagram of his body. The affected areas were coloured in red and a detailed report of his blood pressure, pulse rate, and sugar level were displayed.

Nakul looked tensed as he walked towards the hall. Yudhraj was looking at the screen which displayed the 360-degree view around the ship.

"We are not responsible for anything. We don't owe anyone anything here. Let's get the hell out of this place now," Yudhraj said.

"Set a course back home. Location; from where we started, time from when we left. Now!" Yudhraj commanded Archisa.

"Command accepted! Setting a route back to the origin point," Archisa's voice came through the PA System.

The engine started revving and was ready to take off. Suddenly there was a strong vibration across the floor.

"What's wrong, Archisa?" Yudhraj quickly inquired.

"There seems to be some trouble in pressure launcher," she replied.

"How is that possible? Didn't you detect it before taking off?" Yudhraj asked her again as he looked outside.

"Unfortunately, it wasn't present at that time. Something just hit the launcher outlet of the ship, twelve seconds ago," she said with static disturbance in her sound.

Arjun came forward and picked his bow and arrow, "This isn't right! Our ship can detect attacks from miles away, even when we are in the space, how couldn't she detect this?"

"We...We are under attack. Brace for impact," She announced and the camera detected several arrows flying towards the ship. Though the arrows shot were in a great number, the ship was strong enough to withstand the attack.

After a while the attack stopped, Yudhraj kept looking at the screen to find who attacked them. Few Tribal men came out of the bushes, pointing their arrows and spears towards the ship. One of them held a long pole that had a huge flag at the top. It was something that looked like a Tilak, similar to what Kison had on his forehead.

Bheem scoffed and said, "These fools think they can defeat us with their primitive weapons?" as he walked towards the wall which had a compartment in it. He pressed a button and the compartment opened. He picked up the mace that was kept inside, the same mace he carried everywhere to thwack his enemies. He flexed his arm and picked up the weapon and some portion of it lit up with light as if energy was flowing through it. "I will handle them," he said as he went rushing towards the exit.

"No, wait!" Yudhraj said as he kept monitoring the men outside. "They seem to be in great number; we should plan an attack…" before he could complete his sentence, Bheem opened the door and charged towards the men.

These men looked strong and ruthless; they looked like soldiers who were disguised as tribals. Each one of them had sharp features and well-defined bodies.

Bheem ran towards a bunch of men who quickly fired their arrows towards him. Bheem swung his mace in great force, making the arrows bounce off. He rushed

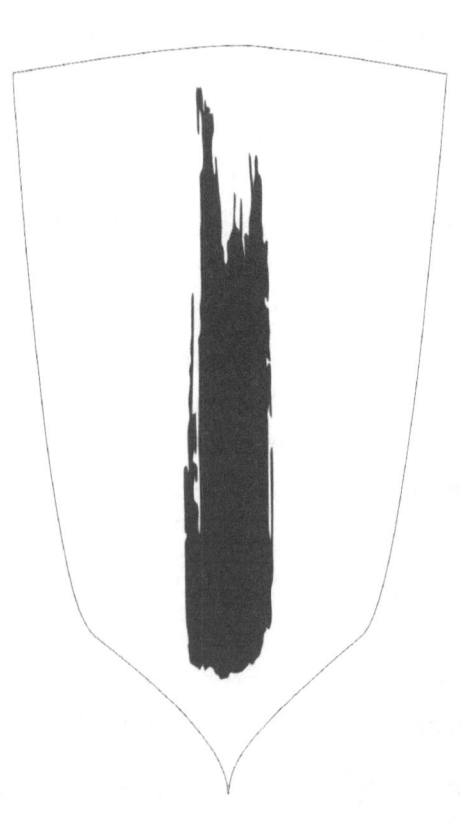

towards them and threw a blow of his mace on the men. In just one blow the men were thrown away and badly injured. Suddenly something came and hit Bheem, he yelled in pain. It was a spear that pierced his back. He couldn't reach it, so he just let it be there and ran towards the man who attacked him and punched his chest so hard that his spine broke out from his back. Everyone around was shocked to see this. One of them yelled out something in a foreign language and everyone started falling back.

"Scared?" Bheem asked, trying to collect his breath.

Bheem wasn't scared of challenges. He could fight innumerable with the same enormous force. Even he didn't know the maximum capacity of his strength. Bheem who was quiet and calm most of the times, could turn into a disastrous monster in blink of an eye.

He stood there panting, covered in the blood of the men he had just bashed.

He realized he was standing in the middle and everyone had surrounded him. There was a huge tree behind him. These men started increasing the gaps between themselves and started moving in an anti-clockwise direction.

Yudhraj, who was observing everything from the ship, was confused to see what was happening.

"What the hell are you guys doing?" Bheem exclaimed!

Suddenly a stone came flying towards Bheem, he realized this and quickly dodged it. The rock went inches away from him and flew exactly between the gaps the men were maintaining.

Arjun yelled, "This is a formation, he doesn't understand."

A skinny man came running out of the gap with a rope in his hand. The man ran in a zigzag towards him, Bheem was confused to see this. The man jumped and cuffed Bheem's right hand, moved towards Bheem's left hand and ran behind him; he was able to pull Bheem's hand towards the left. He then revolved around the tree that was behind him and ran towards Bheem. The rope was falling short, but he promptly cuffed his left hand too. The skinny man ran away and stood at a distance. Everyone pointed their spears towards Bheem who was surrounded by the men from all the sides. Bheem tried to pull away, but as he pulled one hand, the rope pulled his other hand. The harder he pulled, the harder he was bond.

Arjun looked at Yudhraj and said, "Let's get out there; these men aren't amateurs. Open the door," he stood in front of the door, but it did not open.

"What's wrong?" He asked!

"It seems like the door is blocked by something," Archisa replied.

"Blocked by what?" he questioned.

"Show us what's blocking it," Yudhraj commanded.

On the screen, it displayed that the door was blocked by a huge boulder.

"This is crazy," Nakul said as he started panicking.

"This is not the only exit in the ship, I am taking the emergency outlet," and Arjun ran towards his chamber. He stood on a circularly shaped diagram on the floor. The circle quickly opened, and Arjun slid down, but before he could reach the ground outside, he was trapped in a net that covered the outlet.

"What the hell! This was pre-planned!" Arjun grunted as he tried to free himself. He fell down, struggling to get out of the net. He looked at Bheem as he tried to free himself from the cuffs. He knew that this is not a coincidence and they have been attacked with complete planning. It was uncanny how all these things happened right after their tech guy was down and it was planned by someone who knew about the ship's secret exits too, but who would possibly know about this? It was too early for the royal family to attack, and there was no one in the team who could betray.

"STOP!" someone yelled from the woods.

Yudhraj who was trying to find Arjun in the monitoring screens, looked around and saw that someone came walking towards the tree Bheem was tied to. Arjun struggled to see who it was.

Bheem turned around and saw it was Kison!

"You? You did this, didn't you? Untie me and I will rip you apart!" Bheem said in anger as he looked at Kison!

"What the hell?" Nakul exclaimed.

"Everybody calm down!" Kison said in a higher pitch

"Untie him," he commanded.

One of the men came and cut the rope Bheem was tied to. As soon as Bheem was set free, he quickly paced towards Kison.

Kison slid his left foot behind to have a firm stand over the ground. Bheem had already reached close to him with a closed fist to punch him. Bheem threw a punch at Kison, but he effortlessly blocked him with his left hand and pushed him away with his right hand! The push was gentle, but the impact was massive. Bheem couldn't believe that Kison pushed him so effortlessly even though he felt like a thousand rocks were falling on him. He landed far away.

Kison looked how far he went; he took a deep breath and said, "Enough of this nonsense now! You all have been hired to do something, and it is your duty to finish the mission."

Nakul and Yudhraj were quite surprised to see all this happening!

"I am coming inside the ship," Kison announced as he moved towards the entrance.

He slid the huge boulder like it was a feather and the door opened.

He went walking towards the main hall where Nakul and Yudhraj were standing. Yudhraj went a few steps ahead as Kison walked towards them.

"What is going on? We want to abort this mission and we have complete authority to do so" Yudhraj was fuming.

"Authority? On what grounds? Which rule grants you the authority to leave an ongoing mission in the middle? Without informing the person who hired you for the job?" Kison asked as he moved closer to Yudhraj.

Kison, who was always calm, seemed angry now; he looked straight into Yudhraj's eyes as he stood inches away from him.

"You may not know our rules but just for your information, as per the book of code of conduct, rule number 135 Point C, I quote 'The Members are allowed to abort the mission if they aren't given enough resources to finish their task," Yudhraj said as he looked right back at Kison.

Kison had a smirk on his face and said, "The rule number 564 Point E also states that you cannot leave the mission which has involved a guarantee or someone who has challenged a duel on your behalf, right?"

"The biggest mistake one does is to think he knows everything; there is always someone stronger than you. Be prepared," he added.

Yudhraj was scandalized to hear him speak about the code of conduct.

"What? How do you know this? This information is classified, and there is no way you can know this," Yudhraj said as he fumbled.

"That's your cue to believe that I am beyond all this. You are on the greatest mission of your life. You definitely belong to another time zone but let me tell you; you aren't from this world either. This is a different world. I know things you aren't even aware of," Kison said as he looked at Arjun who was standing a few feet away. Beside him was Bheem.

"You want to know the real reason for this mission? Sure! Take your seat this is going to be another long story," Kison said as he looked back at Yudhraj.

There was a pin drop silence in the ship. Everyone sat on their respective seats as Kison looked at them.

Chapter 11

A War Against Adharma

They sat quietly, none of them thought of questioning Kison about the things he knew.

"It's time, I will tell you everything and you will believe it," Kison said as he glanced at all of them.

" The men you fought outside are from the Yadas clan, they are my men, I train them. For the finest warriors in the world, isn't it obvious to you that something is wrong? Your mental and physical strength has been affected by something. Bheem, one of the strongest guy in the universe gets beaten up so easily. Arjun who has a history of killing a thousand men and knows how to handle each and every weapon couldn't figure things out?" Kison said.

He then looked at Arjun with a smirk and said,

"Arjun. You have been part of the 'Universal Assassin's Alliance' you have the capacity to kill over dozen of people single-handedly without any weapon. Your name topped the list of every intergalactic crime-organization. You are their go-to guy, and yet, you couldn't even figure out that there might be a trap waiting for you right outside the exit and you fell for it."

Arjun was terrified to learn that Kison knew so much about him.

"How do you know all this?" He asked.

"Ah, doesn't matter, I know a lot," Kison said as he smiled at him.

Arjun panicked and quickly got off his seat.

"No! This isn't right! This world is way too primitive for you to get this record. In fact, there is no way people of this era know anything about time travel and intergalactic activities. That level of technology cannot exist here, and even if accidentally the tech comes in this time, there is no way one can power it," he said with panic in his voice.

Kison totally ignored Arjun and said,

"Well, moving on! I believe the fact that I know these things, will make you believe me and my intentions. I know each and everything about you. This mission is going to be the greatest mission of your lives. With a track record of 94% victories, I am still not sure if you can win this war."

Yudhraj broke his silence and said, "War? What war?"

"The war against *Adharma*," he replied.

"You all belong to the era of technological advancement but welcome to the era of Magic, Gods and Demons! Reincarnation is not a myth here. A war is coming, a war between right and wrong; a war between good and evil. Though right and wrong are just a matter of perspective, the results are going to change everything. This is a war against *Adharma*," he continued.

Yudhraj interrupted him at the word *Adharma*, "*Adharma*? *Dharma*? We abolished the practise of religion long back in our world. It had done a lot of damage to our ancestors."

Kison had a smile and he replied, "That's what went wrong, rather that's how things went wrong. *Dharma* doesn't have to only mean religion or praying to one God. The real meaning of *Dharma* is reality, faith and belief in something; *Dharma* is doing what you have to do; *Dharma* is believing in the good; *Dharma* is supporting the right."

It took Yudhraj a while to understand the real meaning of *Dharma*, even though he was a person who was already believing in it, without realising that he was.Yudhraj took a deep breath and asked, "We haven't been given any brief before we left, we were given Red Priority and Platinum Grade weapons which is very rare. Why haven't we been told anything about this?"

"This can be your final mission. You all can take retirement, no more killing, no more risking your life for someone you didn't know or care about. You can live your life your way; if someone wants they can spend their life governing a province, others can reunite with their lost sons and everything that they desire."

Arjun stopped listening after he heard Kison say 'lost sons.' He was in a trance.

"Wait! We have literally saved the world so many times. We never got an offer from the organization that stated we would get voluntary retirement. What's so special about this one?" Yudhraj asked.

"This war is going to change the fate of this universe. The outcome of this war is going to change thousands of things; this war involves elements from the past, present, future, devil forces, and things outside this world too. This war will happen, with or without you," Kison replied.

"So, you mean if we leave now the war will still happen? And someone will lose? How did you know that we will be coming here even before it happened? This is very confusing. Please walk me through from the start," Yudhraj said as he was getting irritated.

"I know it all. I know what happened, I know what is happening and I know what will be happening. I am talking in the cosmic sense and not in a general way," Kison replied with a smile.

"What? You know the future, really?" Yudhraj enquired.

Arjun interrupted by saying, "You certainly know things about us, things that even we don't know about each other. How is this possible? When we came here, we detected no technology; we are advanced enough to understand which planet has that potential. How do you know so much about us? And how do you know the future? Because that's not possible unless you are a..." and Arjun abruptly shut his mouth.

"If that helps you, consider me one," Kison replied with his typical smile. The smile of all-knowing.

Nakul had his eyes wide open, "You are a God?" he exclaimed.

"As I said, if that helps you, consider me one! "

Yudhraj however couldn't believe what Kison was inferring; he exclaimed, "No! No! No! Gods don't exist. What are you? Who are you?"

"They call me by many names. Some think I am just lucky, while some think I am a con man that fools people, but there is also a set of people that believe I am a God. For some I am their friend, for someone I am their King, for some I am an enemy but you can call me Kison!" He said and turned around to see that Deva was leaning against the wall. The swelling on his face was still there, but he looked in a better condition.

"I knew it!" Deva said.

"Yes, of course, you know everything. You are born with a gift to understand things even before they unfold themselves. This should have been the first thing that might have crossed your mind when you saw me, right?" Kison asked Deva.

"I wasn't sure. I did a bit of research about this era and figured a few things out. Unfortunately, we cannot check the future as you can, so I don't know how your story ends. This blue-tinted skin, this calm behavior, the way you were planning things and making things happen according to your will, not to forget how effortlessly you fought with all of us. There is no way any normal person can do that, but I also know you have your limitations and hence you cannot fight this war on your own," Deva said as he slowly moved towards kison.

"Yes. I have my limitations. I am a human after all! End of my story? I will die as you all would. I am going to die just like another man in this era would or probably even worse. My death will only come to me after my job is done and that will only be done when your mission is finished," Kison said as he remembered his conversation with Kalki.

Yudhraj sat on his seat and said, "Okay then, let's believe everything you said. We are going against a war with whom?"

"The war is going to be fought against the 100 sons of King Duta," Kison said, but this time he had a rough tone.

"But why? Why is this war necessary? Why break the normal flow of time?" Yudhraj asked.

"Sometimes, it's necessary to break the flow and change fate. The world that will be crafted if they win the war is not worth living in. It is not just the people of this era, but the next hundred generations will suffer. A place where humanity cannot survive. What kind of world that would be? A world with one authority, no freedom, and no free will. A world where things work according to the wish of one person. The idea itself disgusts me; I cannot imagine the future generations living in such a world," Kison replied.

"Okay, so you want us to kill the 100 sons? We will do it. It might take us hardly a day to attack their palace with our ship and in no time everything will turn into dust, this is possible," Yudhraj assured.

"Ah, well, no! You can't attack the palace now. You have challenged the throne," He replied.

"You challenged on our behalf; we didn't even know what was happening," Yudhraj corrected him.

"Still! The war will happen. Do you think killing the 100 sons would be so easy? Remember their birth. If they even come to know about the attack, they are going to unleash demons from hell on you. The great ancestors of King Duta have blessed them with things you have never heard of. The palace is guarded by entities that shall stop you, so don't risk things. Have faith in me. I wish good for all of you," and Kison placed his hand on Yudhraj's shoulder for assurance.

Deva looked at Kison and said, "You want this war to happen. You want the bloodshed to happen. You want that things should end on a battlefield and not across the table. You want all of them to die."

"Maybe that's the only solution to stop this madness? Maybe the battle might start across the table and end on the battlefield?" Kison said mysteriously.

Yudhraj cleared his throat and said, "Okay then. How do we stop this so-called madness?"

"To begin with, fight the duel that is in the next three days. Prepare yourself to fight against enemies you aren't aware of. They might be primitive, but there is a high chance that they might defeat you all. This duel is going to set a lot of things in place. So yes, next move, win the duel," Kison said as he moved towards the exit.

"I think I have given you enough information that will restrict your departure. Win this war and you will have an amazing life waiting for you," he said as the exit door opened.

"Give your best; the war is coming," his voice faded as he left the ship.

There was a pin drop silence in the ship, Yudhraj broke the silence and said, "Not for the last mission, but let's finish this! Let's get back to the world we deserve."

Everyone got off their seats and walked towards their chambers.

A God? A lucky man? Who was Kison? Was he really the reincarnation of some God? Or just someone from another timeline, trying to fix things in this one. Everyone had the same doubt. Everyone entered the pod and went off to sleep. They all had their doubts, but one thing was sure there was a war coming, one way or another.

Chapter 12

The Duel Begins

King Duta was in his meditation room, chanting, "Om Namah Shivaay."

Sage Vyaan opened the door and walked inside.

"So, here you are," he said, looking at the King trying to meditate with a lot of efforts.

"Yes," King whispered slowly.

"My King, the principle of meditation is to forget everything and be one with the Supreme Being. You cannot reach your full potential until you don't let go off things. You might be meditating, but there are a thousand thoughts running in your head and those are barricades that are stopping you from being free of the world and its desires," he said.

King got up from his place, flexed his arms and said, "No one knows that better than you, but how do I calm my mind? The mind that knows something wrong is about to happen today. Kison is not the person who makes a mistake; he challenged my sons on behalf of the men. We don't even know who they are or what they are capable of. We have never seen them in the kingdom they are probably from some different place."

"Probably my King, but you know we have things that can stop them. Things we aren't proud of, but we must do whatever it takes to keep the throne in our family," Vyaan said in a low voice.

"No. I have never used those grants ever in my life, I have fought more than a thousand battles and never have I thought of using them because the moment we utilize those sources we owe those entities," King said as he stared at the floor with his blind eyes.

It was his shame that hung his head. He could do anything to make his sons win this duel because he knew. Kison wouldn't play a losing side and if Kison supports something he knows it is winning. He was one of the smartest and strongest men he ever encountered. Kison had been loyal to him for a very long time. The King knew Kison had no greed for the kingdom; he was also aware of the fact that Kison was very powerful. The only reason why Kison stood by his side till now was that he believed that he was a just King, but now the King was scared, very scared.

"My King, let us trust our princes. They have been trained by the best and cannot be defeated easily. They have fought many battles and haven't lost any yet. Let's see what happens today," Sage Vyaan said.

"Commander Vidurm is not here yet, he has gone to the north, but when he returns, I am sure he will be of great assistance," He added.

Meanwhile in the ship...

Nakul tip-toed around the ship. He walked with extra caution so that nobody notices his movements. He stood outside Deva's chamber.

He touched his coms and said,

"Hey Deva, buddy! Where are you at?"

"I am in the power room. Why? You need something?"

"Ah! no, actually I wanted to grab a snack, thought I would ask you for some."

"Have fun Nakul, let me work."

And Deva cut the connections off.

Nakul left a huge sigh of relief and entered Deva's chambers.

As he walked inside, one by one, all the lights lit up.

He saw that there were five mannequins that were dressed with astonishing armours.

"Scammy Kammy! I knew this guy was working on something amazing," Nakul said as he tried to control his excitement.

He felt someone was standing near the door and he quickly turned around to see who it was.

"What are you doing here?" Bheem asked as he was standing outside Deva's chamber trying to understand why Nakul would sneak into someone's chamber like this.

"Oh! Brother! When did you come here?" Nakul questioned as he tried hard to act normal.

"I followed you while you were dramatically walking on your toes trying not to make noise which caught my attention even more," he replied.

"Yeah Yeah," Nakul said as he scratched his head in embarrassment.

He took a small pause and continued, "Look around you; he made us new armours. They look so cool. So different from what we have used till now."

Bheem glanced around and found proficiently crafted armours worn by the mannequins.

"So this is what he was doing for so long," Bheem said to himself as he looked at how thoughtfully the armours were constructed.

"Man, I thought he was in depression or something. I sent him some jokes, but he hasn't even opened my texts till now, however, I am glad he was busy making these armours and not crying over something," Nakul said as he went near one of the armours.

Deva found out that the door of his chamber was open and he rushed to see what was happening.

"Hey! You are not allowed to see that yet," he yelled at Bheem and Nakul as he stood outside his chamber.

Both of them were startled as they heard Deva's voice.

"I just followed Nakul, his activity seemed suspicious," Bheem said quickly.

Nakul instantly moved towards him as he heard the word 'suspicious', "What do you mean by suspicious? Am I here to steal something, huh?" he questioned like a child.

Bheem looked back at him and asked, "My chocolate cookies go missing every time I leave my room, rings any bell?"

Nakul fake laughed and turned away from Bheem to avoid the conversation, as he had been sneaking into Bheem's room and stealing his snacks.

"Excuse me? Can we get back to the real issue over here?" Deva interrupted as he found the current conversation futile.

Listening to the argument, Arjun and Yudhraj reached Deva's chamber.

"What's going on?" Yudhraj asked as he entered the chamber.

He looked around and noticed the armours; he was amused to see the work of craft Deva did.

"Mind-blowing," Yudhraj whispered.

Arjun stood at his place, observing the armours.

Deva kept the toolbox on the ground and stood in front of them.

"Okay! I have been working over something for a while. The reason why nobody knows about this is that I didn't want unnecessary feedback from immature folks here," and he looked at Nakul.

"What?" Nakul grunted.

Deva ignored him and continued, "I have designed these armours with a lot of thought in my mind. The design is what matches the current period. The dynamics are planned in a way that would add grace to the armours. These armours are concocted as per an individual's skill sets. So that everybody can do whatever they are good at. They are still in prototype mode and I am not sure how effective they would be in today's duel."

Everyone was impressed by Deva's skills and expertise. Deva has always been the reason behind efficient back-end. They won half of their fights with Deva on his chair, sitting in front of giant computer screens figuring things out.

"These armours will be synced with your badges after I program them, so they will automatically fit your body," he said as he checked the screen that displayed some infographics.

"Let's try these in the training room," Deva said, looking at the hologram on the other end.

TRAINING ROOM.

It was a huge empty room that had hard walls. The training room was that part of the ship where they all trained for battles and tested new weapons.

Everybody stood side by side, and the suits were placed in a pod. There were separate compartments for all the suits.

Deva pressed a button and the lids of all the compartments opened at once.

Each suit got dismantled into different parts and levitated towards their respective owners. All the parts were positioned on the right part of the body.

The armours looked perfect.

Nakul looked at his suit and screamed, "Looks like somebody is going to win today!"

The armours were quintessential; they were the best of both worlds. Looked like traditional armours while they had everything the advanced civilization could add. Heavy-duty, as well as comfortable at the same time. Each one of them had their favourite weapon customized to the suit. Yudhraj had an energy shield and light saber sword, Nakul had a spear which had a sharp red crystal on its head and long blades, Bheem had his mace and Arjun had a bow that seemed to be capable of firing more than just arrows.

Deva looked at the armours; he raised his hand and from his gauntlet came out another holographic projection that stated-

'Impact resistant

Shock Absorbent

Water Resistant

GPS Tracker

Body Structure Compatibility

Contingency opt-out'

Besides these, other dozens of things were mentioned too.

The screen in that room displayed Kison standing outside the ship, waiting for the door to open.

"Alright, let's go see what he has to say," Yudhraj said as he realized it was about time they left for the duel.

They all marched towards the assembly hall, wearing the armours, the main door of the ship opened and Kison walked in.

"Are you going to fight with these?" Kison questioned as he looked at their high tech exoskeletons.

"Yes!" Yudhraj said firmly.

"No! You cannot let people know about time travel, even if a part of your tech is discovered by the people of this era; it's going to create a crack in the timeline. People are still not aware of time travel, even if one gets to know it's going to change the course of history," Kison said

"Then what do we do? Fight with what?" Yudhraj inquired.

Kison looked at him and calmly said, "Weapons of this era."

Arjun interrupted as he heard this, "With all due respect. We can finish this much faster if we use our weapons."

"Not happening, I cannot let you use the technology that is thousands of years far from these men. I know what happens when someone gets hold of such tech," he replied.

This caught Deva's attention, and he asked, "Do You? Does it cause a paradox?"

Nakul interrupted by saying, "Um, aren't we supposed to not talk about time travel? Even talking about time travel creates some problem, right? Let's just do as he says. We can still win this without our weapons."

"Alright then, you will get your weapons when you reach the arena. This is part of the procedure to avoid people from tampering with the weapons," Kison said

Deva pressed a button and everyone's armours were dismantled and levitated back to the pod.

Everyone was back to their skin suits.

"Also another problem, you cannot dress like this either, you have to wear traditional attire. As you reach there, you shall get your armours. They are pretty effective, to keep you alive during the battle," he added.

"I don't think we will be comfortable with your armour, we are used to nanotechnology, our clothes and even our suits are part of our bodies. The nano-particles come out and cover our body with the kind of outfit we want. So even if it's heavy duty armour, it feels very comfortable," Yudhraj said as he pointed towards the gadget on his chest that helped them transform.

Deva came ahead and said, "Yudhraj, I think let's not try the new armours now, we are yet to test them. I am not sure if they are 100% full proof. We really need a test run."

"Yes, do it when you come back," Kison said.

"Come back?" Deva whispered as he heard Kison say that.

Kison winked at him and walked towards the exit.

Deva left a sigh and everyone went to their respective chambers to change their outfits.

A while later, everyone came out dressed in the traditional attires.

"Let's go!" Kison said as he walked out of the ship.

They reached the arena where the fight was supposed to take place. There was a lot of cheering and excitement going on, people had gathered in huge number to watch the duel.

"Is this some kinda festival?" Nakul asked as he saw all the people.

The area was huge in a circular format; there was a sandy field in between and around it there was a multi-level seating for people to sit and watch the duels. There were four gates across the border.

There was an area reserved on the first storey where the royal family could sit and watch the duels.

"Follow me," Kison said as he walked towards a staircase that went underground, everyone followed him. They ended near the door of a small room, Kison opened it and went inside. There was a huge window and from there, the entire battlefield was visible. Many weapons were mounted on the wall nearby. Weapons such as swords, sabers, daggers, spears, bow and arrows, mace and different kinds of shields.

"Pick your weapon, you will find the suitable armour over there," and pointed towards another wall where armours of different shapes were placed.

"Try them out and choose whatever fits," he said as he walked outside the room.

"Where are you going?" Yudhraj asked him

"I am not supposed to be around you before the battle starts. I will be watching you all. All the best. Remember this battle is going to put a lot of things in order," he said as he walked away.

Everyone exchanged a look and started preparing for the battle.

"So? Who goes first?" Nakul asked.

"I will," Bheem said promptly

"My last encounter wasn't really great, this time I will fight him and finish this," he added as he popped his knuckles.

Yudhraj went near Bheem and said, "Sure, we don't know what we are up against. The story of their birth runs chills down my spine. You are the strongest and I am sure you can defeat whoever is against you but remember to stay calm and composed," and he patted his shoulder.

Bheem looked at the veins in his body that popped out and were black in colour; he then picked up the largest sized armour and wore it. He looked around to see if he could find a mace and he found a rusty one. He picked it up and swung it in the air.

"This doesn't seem too bad. The grip is a little iffy, but it works for me," he said to himself as he kept on swinging the mace in the air.

A man opened the door; he had a shield in one and spade in another.

"The duel is about to start, who is coming?" he asked in a dry tone.

"Me," Bheem said as he walked towards the man.

"All the best my man," Nakul exclaimed.

Bheem went walking towards the battlefield through a tunnel that ended near its entrance.

He saw thousands of people staring at him and from the end came out Diyohan! He too held a mace in his hand, but it was golden and looked in a much better state.

As soon as he set his foot on the ground, everyone started cheering for him.

Diyohan wore his royal armour that had artistic engravings on it.

The rest of them were in the room from where they could spectate everything.

Kison sat next to the King.

A person standing at the corner blew the conch thrice and the cheers became even louder.

Both of them charged against each other with great speed holding their mace with a firm grip.

Chapter 13

The Black Veins

Diyohan punched Bheem so hard that it nearly broke his face. He instantly fell on the ground, while Diyohan took a few steps back to catch his breath. Bheem stood up with the help of his mace and looked at Diyohan.

"So, that's all you got?" Bheem mocked him.

"I just got started," Diyohan said as he charged towards Bheem.

This time Bheem dodged his attack, it was unlikely of Bheem to not be aggressive in a fight and act defensive, but he understood it would be easier for him to fight this way.

There was a man standing next to the King; he kept on telling the blind King about everything that was happening. Move by move, second by second. He wore a combination of orange & green robe and a white dhoti. The artistically embroidered turban on his head suited his magnificent beard and moustache. His eyes were lit up as he narrated everything to the King. His name was Nayanraj.

Nayanraj had the gift of 'Divine Vision;' he could see things happening at far, not just from one angle

but multiple angles. He could zoom in and zoom out anywhere he wanted; he had his eyes everywhere. His eyes were shining and illuminating light, the innumerable uneven glowing colourful spots in his eyes looked like several solar systems had somehow melted into one.

"Nayanraj! Why did you stop?" the King asked him

"Nothing to worry about my Highness, there is a slight change in the course of action, but I am sure Prince Diyohan is still going to get him," he said.

Bheem stepped back as he assessed Diyohan!

"Come on! Fight me!" Diyohan provoked him.

"Sure!" Bheem said as he moved one step at a time, sideways, looking straight into his eyes.

Bheem quickly moved towards Diyohan and swung his mace upwards to hit him with an uppercut. Diyohan instantly tried to block Bheem's attack with his mace. Before Diyohan could block his move, Bheem abruptly controlled the force of his mace. Instead of swinging the mace upwards, he lowered it and attacked Diyohan's torso.

The impact was powerful enough for Diyohan to lose his balance.

"Impressive," Diyohan said while he was trying to hide his pain.

Bheem swung his mace again and hammered him on the same spot even before Diyohan could see it coming.

The armour now had a crack on it.

Diyohan coughed as the impact was strong and direct.

Before Diyohan could catch his breath, Bheem hurried towards him and shoulder pushed him with all his strength. The push was so strong that Diyohan lost his balance and fell a few feet away. Bheem didn't stop; he ran towards him, jumped in the air to smash Diyohan's head with his mace. He swung down the mace with great force, within a blink of an eye, the mace that was little far above him almost reached Diyohan's face. Diyohan saw that the mace rapidly moved towards him and his face was about to get smashed by the heavy globe but he instantly blocked the attack with his palm. It was effortless, and it didn't even feel like he blocked a great blow. Bheem was flabbergasted by the strength of Diyohan.

Everyone in the arena was shocked to see how easily Diyohan blocked this attack.

Yudhraj and the men were shocked too.

"What? This is impossible," Yudhraj exclaimed.

"It looks like he was just trying to understand the maximum capacity of Bheem," Arjun replied as he looked at the duel.

Bheem took a step back to figure out Diyohan's next move.

Diyohan raised both his legs and plunged towards Bheem to kick him, the kick landed on his chest and Bheem fell on the ground.

The kick was so impactful that Bheem's armour broke.

Bheem steadily got back on his feet. He saw that his armour was now damaged and it would do more harm than good. It broke in the middle and exposed his chest. The broken edges could tear through his chest easily.

He put his fingers in the gap and pulled the armour until it made some space for his huge fists to make their way in. He then viciously ripped the armour apart.

Bheem literally tore an armour made of iron with his bare hands and it put everyone in shock. He threw one piece on the left side and other on the right. Someone from the crowd cheered and everyone followed him.

He stood there with his bare chest. Bheem had a huge body, his dreads covered his back. His muscles looked as strong as a rock and had cuts in perfect proportion. His veins popped out and were visible because they were almost black.

Nayanraj stopped his narration again and glanced at Bheem to see why his veins looked black.

"What is it, Nayanraj?" the King asked him again.

"My King! Stop this battle right now," Nayanraj quickly replied.

"What? Why would you say that?" the King asked cluelessly.

Nayanraj quickly turned towards Sage Vyaan.

"You see that?"

"Yes! But I am not sure if what I see is real or not," Vyaan replied.

"What are you seeing? Tell me now," the King demanded.

Nayanraj ignored what the King said and continued talking to Sage Vyaan.

"Sage! If it is what we think it is, then we have to stop this battle now. We cannot risk what might happen next, his transformation can cause havoc here," Nayanraj said as he seemed extremely stressed.

"I command you to tell me what is happening," The King commanded in a firm voice.

"My King, what we see here is, this man has black veins all over his body,"

"Black veins? You mean like the way it is written in the stories?" the King asked.

The Queen who was seated beside him all this time finally broke her silence and yelled out, "What? Stop this battle right now!"

"We cannot stop the battle now. It is against the rules," the King said even though he was worried about his son.

"Yes my King, but how is it possible. We have been looking for someone who could withstand this and nobody could ever do that till now! How could he do that?" interjected Nayanraj.

The Queen was visibly stressed after listening to everything Nayanraj narrated.

Bheem and Diyohan both engaged in hand-to-hand combat. Both of them threw punches at each other and kept hitting until the blood sprinkled in all directions.

None of them was ready to back out; both fought for a very long time.

Bheem abruptly stopped and faced his back towards Diyohan.

Diyohan couldn't understand what was happening, Bheem seemed in pain. He growled out loud. His veins started moving as if something was flowing through them and knots began forming on his body.

"It is happening," Yudhraj said as he looked at what was going on.

"If he is unable to control this, rest in peace Diyohan!" Nakul exclaimed.

Bheem screamed out as the knots started increasing on his body.

"My King, he is transforming!" Nayanraj exclaimed.

Suddenly Bheem stopped yelling, stood still a for few seconds and fell straight on the ground.

"What just happened?" Yudhraj asked as he was shocked to see Bheem falling.

Nakul came in front to get a clear view and he said, "Followed by the growling comes the destruction. But why isn't he transforming? Why is he on the ground?"

Everyone was shocked to see what just happened.

Vyaan looked around to find Kison; he noticed that Kison quickly sat back on his seat and left a sigh.

"What happened to him?" Vyaan asked Kison.

"What did I miss? I had to relieve myself."

"We are going to talk about this later on," Vyaan said.

"Sure," Kison replied as he looked at the battlefield.

Bheem was on the ground, motionless but his eyes blinked. He blinked harder to stay conscious. His eyesight started to get blurry and everything started distorting. The voice echoed and faded away as he tried to keep his eyes open.

Bheem was not an ordinary man. His black veins weren't a disorder or some disease. Bheem belonged to the doorkeepers family, because of the way they were built.

Bheem tried his best to remain conscious, but with every blink, it was becoming harder and he finally passed out.

FLASHBACK

Bheem opened his eyes and found himself tied to a heavy metal log that was drowning in the water. He felt extremely sick and weak. With whatever energy he had, he tried to free himself, but his efforts didn't help him. At last, he gave up and closed his eyes to accept his death in this barbaric manner. For the last time, he opened his eyes, hoping for a miracle to save him.He saw a huge snake pacing towards him, he panicked and yelled but couldn't do anything. The huge snake bit him on his hand and Bheem instantly fell unconscious.

Bheem opened his eyes and noticed he was on the land, but this looked different. No neon lights, no hovering cars or no gliding bikes. It was a cave that was dark.

Bheem got back on his feet; he felt better than what he felt while he was drowning. Bheem turned around and saw a bunch of men pointing their guns towards him.

"Relax! I don't want any trouble. How did I get here?" he asked as he raised his hands in the air to surrender.

A man came walking from behind.

"Everybody, lower your weapons!"

"Who are you, and what place is this?" Bheem questioned him.

"I am Bhujangketu and welcome to *Bhujangnagari!*"

Bhujangketu was an old man who held a staff in his hand, he spoke softly but had great depth in his voice

"What place is this?" Bheem asked again

"I think there is something more important than this question," Bhujangketu replied.

"What is it?"

"You were drowning and then you were bitten by a snake and yet you survived? Do you know what had happened to you? And what bit you?" he questioned.

"I was in a fight with some intruders and they attacked me with something and I felt dizzy. After that, I don't remember anything. The next thing I remember is drowning and finally, a huge snake attacking me," Bheem replied as he looked at the unfamiliar faces around.

"You were poisoned with synthetic venom that is made in the labs and later you were bitten by a deadly poisonous snake," Bhujangketu said.

"What?" Bheem exclaimed.

"There is no way any normal human species can survive this! You have to be one of us."

"One of you?"

"Yes!" He said and moved towards Bheem.

Bhujangketu's back started forming knots and soon his body was covered with them. His veins popped out and the clots turned green in color and he transformed into a different creature. Snake scales started appearing on his body; the upper body turned into something that looked like a combination of snake and a man.

"What the hell is this?" Bheem yelled in panic.

Chapter 14
The Warmonger

Diyohan kept looking at Bheem as he lay motionless on the ground. He went near Bheem, placed his feet below his chest, and rolled him over. He lay unconscious on the ground and his face was covered with dirt. Diyohan with his feet, moved Bheem's face to make sure he wasn't playing dead.

"That's all? You scream in pain and then you go to sleep?" Diyohan asked as he looked down at the unconscious Bheem.

He turned towards the crowd and asked them, "Do you want me to spare his life? Or Finish him?"

"Finish him! Finish him!" chanted the people.

"Alright then, let's finish him!" Diyohan exclaimed as he clenched his fist.

He sat on his knees and threw hard blows on Bheem's face. He started at slow speed, but gradually the speed increased and he didn't stop until he was exhausted.

He got up, covered in Bheem's blood. He yelled in victory and his people cheered him on.

Yudhraj couldn't understand this.

"Something is wrong! He cannot be beaten so easily," said Yudhraj.

"I know, but it happened," Arjun said in a whisper.

Far from the seating area at the very top of the battlefield, Bhishmaji and Dronaji stood watching everything.

"Did you do something?" Bhishmaji asked Dronaji.

"Nothing, I am as surprised as you are," he replied.

Nayanraj narrated everything to the King as he wondered what happened.

Nayanraj looked at Kison from the corner of his eye and he observed that he didn't take part in the conversation.

Kison looked back at Nayanraj and said, "What? I didn't even see what happened."

"Sure! What do I know, even I did not see anything," he said as he emphasized on the word 'see.'

Diyohan was declared as the winner!

The entire stadium yelled, "Diyohan! Diyohan! Diyohan!"

Two men came, held both the hands of Bheem and dragged his heavy body out of the battlefield. They dragged him towards the room where the other men were. They opened the door and threw him inside.

Deva rushed to see what had happened to Bheem and why wasn't he moving.

"He is breathing," Deva said in relief.

"Why isn't he moving?" Nakul questioned.

"I don't know, give me a minute," Deva said as he pulled something out of his back pocket.

Yudhraj looked at what Deva pulled out and exclaimed, "Wait! what? Did you bring a tech here? We were told not to bring any techs, right?"

"I know, but this is fine," he said as he held a small rectangular device in his hand which was metallic and had a small circle in between. It had a lens at the center. Deva pointed the lens towards Bheem and a light came out of the lens and scanned him. A hologram was projected from the small circle that was in the center. It displayed a couple of figures and some textual information.

'Subject Name: Bheem

Status: Unconscious

Physical Damage: 86%

Mental Damage: 41%

Injuries: Fracture, Ligament Tear, Muscle Damage and Temporary Paralysis due to Poisoning.'

"Temporary Paralysis due to poisoning, what poison?" Deva asked the device.

The previous stats were cleared and a new holographic screen popped out.

'Name of the poison: Jurgsin

Components: Made out of larkspur plant.

Effect: Temporary

Damage: Mild

Healing time: 2-3 Hours

After effects: Nausea

Affected Area: Neck'

As soon as Deva read this, he quickly put the device in his back pocket and turned Bheem around.

They all saw that a very thin needle had pierced through Bheem's neck. Deva carefully pulled out the pin and threw it away.

"He should be fine within 2-3 hours," Deva said as he looked at the motionless Bheem.

Yudhraj and Arjun looked at each other as a series of questions raced in their minds.

"Arjun, when did this happen?" Yudhraj asked.

"I have no idea! I didn't see Diyohan doing this."

"Maybe we missed it? Otherwise, how is it possible that he was attacked with a needle?" doubts rose in Yudhraj's mind.

Nakul looked at Bheem for a few moments, he quickly turned towards Yudhraj and said, "Maybe, someone fired it towards him from a distance?"

"High possibility," Arjun backed Nakul's opinion.

"But with what? The needle is thinner than a straw of haystack and miniature launchers aren't here yet so how?" Arjun asked himself.

Deva was observing Bheem's wound carefully.

"It has gone pretty deep, the needle is long and considering how thick his skin is, it has been fired with 100% accuracy to hit the softest part of the neck. What are your thoughts on this Arjun?" he asked.

"It's possible, but it's hard to understand how far it was fired from. Accuracy is impeccable."

Suddenly they all noticed that Kison was standing near the door.

"What happened to him?" Kison asked

Deva told him about the needle they found but didn't disclose the device.

"We will get to the roots of this after the duel ends, who goes next?" He asked.

Arjun stepped forward, but before he could say anything, Nakul took a step ahead and said, "Let me go, this is cheating. We clearly know that it's interference from some third party and with such things happening, we cannot fight them. Arjun is our best shot and we can't use him until we know what all they are capable of. Earlier it was a needle, this time we don't know what it can be. I will enter the rink," Nakul said as he picked up a spear which was on the ground.

Arjun looked at him and said, "Are you sure?"

"Most definitely," he replied.

Yudhraj turned around to see who was next and he saw Dushan walking in the middle of the battlefield with a glove that extended till this elbow. It had two thick whips attached to it.

"Whips," Yudhraj chuckled. "Go Nakul," he said in encouraging voice.

Kison too saw who it was and said "He isn't Dushan, he is one of the clones but don't consider him less powerful than the real one."

"Sure!" Nakul said as he picked up a maroon colored armour and left the room.

Nakul might be a fun loving guy, but he was a warmonger, he kept his calm during the fight and played while he fought the enemy. He yelled and screamed in joy as he broke bones and pulled out organs during the battles. He laughed while he fought; this irritated his opponent the most. But this time he was a bit angry, he knew he had to win this battle if not for anything else but for Bheem, who was knocked down with unfair means.

Nakul stepped in the battlefield and saw Dushan already standing in the middle.

Nakul approached him with a very angry face; he paced towards him, but abruptly stopped and smiled at Dushan.

Dushan didn't understand what was happening.

Nakul dropped his Spear on the ground, removed his headgear and threw it on the other side.

"What is he doing?" Yudhraj asked himself.

Nakul looked around and saw the crowd was silent.

"Okay, you all are silent now. Had to do something that would maintain some silence in here! Now that you all are quite, I want to introduce myself! I am Nakul and I am going to win this fight. This baldy cannot defeat me; he can't even grow hair over his head!" Nakul exclaimed

"Ohh," the crowd whispered gently.

He then picked up his headgear and his Spear.

"Let's do this?" he asked Dushan.

"Sure!" Dushan said as he started swinging his whips in the air.

Kison looked at Nakul and said, "Come on, throw some colors Nakul."

Nakul threw his Spear towards Dushan and leaped in the air towards him. The Spear wasn't thrown with force, so it did not travel swiftly. As he was in the air he caught the Spear before it could hit Dushan, he took a spin in the air and hit Dushan's face with the other end of the Spear.

Dushan wasn't expecting something like this.

Dronaji looked at Bhishmaji and said, "This move reminds me of you."

"I know! This is my move, and I haven't used it anywhere other than our practice sessions. How is this possible?" Bhishmaji said as he was confused to see someone copying his undisclosed moves.

Dushan slashed his whip on the ground and looked at Nakul; he was standing a few feet away. He whipped another one towards Nakul; it rolled around Nakul's left hand and as soon as it did Dushan pulled him with great force. The pull was extremely firm; Nakul was drawn towards him. Dushan clenched his fist to punch him.

Nakul was just a meter away from Dushan, he was about to punch him when suddenly Nakul pulled his Spear and stabbed Dushan in his stomach.

There was a gasp in the entire stadium; everyone went quiet.

The Spear went through Dushan and blood continuously dripped out. Nakul grabbed Dushan's armour and pulled out the Spear and pierced it on the ground.

"Thank you, everyone! That's all folks," He said.

The King broke in to tears as he heard this.

"Did that really happen?"

Queen Gundhi sat silently as she tried to fathom what was going on.

Nayanraj left a sigh and said, "Sorry to say this King, but one of your sons is dead. To my surprise, this happened too quickly; the fight didn't even last for a few minutes."

Nakul tried to locate where Diyohan was sitting, and after a while, he found him. He was sitting on the second lane on his huge chair that was made of granite.

"Yo, Diyohan! My man Bheem could have killed you the same way, only if you guys didn't cheat." he yelled at the top of his voice.

"What cheating?" he yelled back.

"As if you don't know?"

"Crawl back to your dungeon and celebrate your victory," Diyohan yelled louder.

"Man, I am just getting started! Do you have more of these fake vessel-made clones? Send them here so I can put all of them down," he said as he pointed out towards the dead body of the clone.

"How dare you?" Virakanna finally broke his silence.

"Oh! Brother to the rescue, but wait are you even real? Or another clone?" Nakul mocked.

Virakanna raised his fist and pointed his finger towards Nakul and yelled, "SMASH."

Nakul failed to understand the intentions of Virakanna.

Yudhraj paid keen attention to what was happening.

"What is happening?" he asked Arjun

"I don't know."

Suddenly huge boulders came flying from every direction and fell on Nakul.

The falling of boulders made dust fly everywhere.

Virakanna yelled, "I am real and alive; you might be real but not alive anymore."

The place where Nakul stood was now covered with the ruins of the boulders.

"My King, Virakanna smashed him under the boulders," Nayanraj said to the King.

Vyaan looked at Kison; he was calm and didn't react.

"Something is not right," Vyaan whispered to himself.

The crowd fell silent after seeing this; it was dust all over the place. Suddenly everyone felt a mild tremor. The broken boulders started shaking and something lit inside the heap. The light was bright, vibrant and colorful, all of a sudden, the rocks were tossed up in the sky and something flew out with great force and landed in front of Virakanna!

It was Nakul! He was glowing and had a colorful aura around him; it looked like energy flowed through him. His eyes were lit up with the bright, colorful lights, and he was levitating above the ground.

"Mistake!" Nakul said.

He was not loud, but his voice echoed in the entire stadium.

Chapter 15

Celestials

The King jumped off his seat "What voice is this?" he asked.

Nayanraj was shocked just like the others to see the entire scene. Nakul's magnified voice sent chills down everyone's spine.

"Withdraw the battle, my King," Nayanraj stammered.

"Kison! Who is he?" he exclaimed.

"I am as surprised as you are, my King. This is new," Kison said as he got up from his seat.

Everyone looked at him with disbelief.

Dronaji and Bhishmaji looked at each other and were shocked too.

Nayanraj's eyes light up a little brighter as he tried to look at Nakul.

"My King! He...He...He is a 'celestial' this cannot happen," Nayanraj said as he looked at Nakul.

"Impossible! You should have sensed it way before, if he was one of you," the King said.

"Yes! But I don't know who he is, I have never seen him

in the Celestial Realm nor does he belong to any of the clusters. And I am so sure about this because none of us is this strong, his energy levels are unmatched. Never in my life have I witnessed such an energy surge," Nayanraj said looking frightened.

Nakul held Virakanna by his royal coat and threw him in the rink. Nakul was hovering in the air, he turned and glided towards him.

Virakanna was on the ground and saw Nakul coming at him. Virakanna was terrified to see a man floating in mid-air. The bright light coming out his body, the aura behind him, his lit up eyes made Virakanna incapable of moving.

He crawled backward as he saw Nakul approaching him.

"So is this how you defeated Bheem? By using weapons?" Nakul asked, and his voice had layers to it, it seemed like a couple of men spoke along with him. There was variation, but it was in a unison.

"I don't know what you are talking about," Virakanna said as he tried to get away from the angry Nakul.

Nakul landed on his feet and walked towards him. As he lay his foot on the ground, the dust around his feet floated into the air. Virakanna stood up and looked at him helplessly; he dusted off the dirt on his coat and stared at Nakul.

Nakul hovered in the air again, his fist lit up with bright light and he took a flight towards Virakanna with great speed. He clenched his fist and aimed to punch him in the face. The flight was so quick that hardly anybody could see Nakul. All they saw was a wind blowing towards Virakanna. Nakul's fist was just about to hit Virakanna and break the very existence of atoms and molecules in him when Kison suddenly appeared to be standing in between them and blocked Nakul's punch with his open palm.

As soon as Nakul's fist collided with Kison's palm, a huge explosion of light was caused, followed by a very strong wave of force coming from the center. The energy was so strong that Virakanna was thrown far away. The walls of the stadium cracked and the giant trees outside the stadium were uprooted. There was a lot of dust in the air; it took a little time for the dust to settle.

Virakanna was totally unaware of what had happened. The force threw him far away.

The dust settled and everyone saw that Kison was holding Nakul's fist firmly, the place where they stood was destroyed, and there was a depression in the ground.

Yudhraj was shocked to see this.

"Kison blocked Nakul's sonic punch with his open palm," he exclaimed in surprise as he couldn't believe what he saw.

Deva looked into his device and said "I can see that, but there is something else you might want to see," as he showed the holographic information to Yudhraj and Arjun.

"WHAT!" both of them exclaimed in surprise.

"What does this even mean?" Yudhraj asked.

"This is strange," Deva replied.

The device displayed:

'Subjects detected: 1

No major damage caused minor bruises and increased Heart Beats.

2 Corpse detected

No more available data.'

They quickly turned towards the rink and saw that Kison and Nakul were standing in the same position and didn't move.

"Why aren't they moving?" Yudhraj asked himself.

"I think we should get there and see what's happening," Arjun muttered.

There was a pin drop silence in the crowd; everyone was trying to understand what was happening. Nakul and Kison were frozen like they were some statues.

Yudhraj reached the rink and walked towards Nakul. His body was stiff, his eyes didn't blink, and neither did Kison's. It was like time froze for both of them.

Nayanraj finished explaining everything to the King and added, "Kison stopped it my King."

"Who else could!" the King replied.

Somewhere else…

Nakul opened his eyes and found himself in a dark empty space. It was endless and quiet. He looked around to see where he was and saw Kison standing behind him.

"Scammy Kammy! You are creepy. What are we doing here?" He asked.

"You were about to attack Virakanna with the sonic punch, if you remember?"

"I do, but wait! you stopped me. How?" He asked.

"Do you realize the amount of energy you produced and used to punch a mere mortal?" Kison asked, completely ignoring his question.

"So what man? He threw boulders at me. If it wasn't me, someone else would have died."

"Doesn't justify. Your species is highly advanced even for the time you belong to. Your energy is concomitant to the universe you are in. Using unbalanced energy will not only break the flow of energy but will attract problems people aren't ready for. You yourself aren't ready to fight, if something comes to this planet. You are only supposed to use these powers where it's required or at places where no harm can be caused," Kison said.

"How do you know that?" Nakul asked as he was astonished to hear Kison knowing so much about him.

"You belong to the highest energies, don't waste it here. I can't let you do that!" Kison said firmly.

"Yeah? And how are you gonna stop me?" Nakul asked as he tried to get back to the rink.

Kison went near him and gently tapped his forehead. Nakul's eyes lit up, and his jaw dropped.

Elsewhere...

Nakul looked at his hands, and they were tiny. He looked around and saw he was in a golden fortress.

"There is my baby boy," a man said. He had long dreads tied as a bun on his head. He wore a maroon cloak, long white shirt, black leather pants and black boots.

He approached Nakul and picked him up in his arms.

"Had a good sleep?"

"Yes, daddy!" Nakul replied.

His dad took him near the window, as he looked outside, Nakul could see the whole universe. His dad pointed a finger outside and the directions of the stars changed, meteors showered and planets came into existence. He did another hand sign and a solar system was formed. He channelized the energy flow of the solar system and created stars.

"Someday, even you can do this," he said to Nakul as baby Nakul enjoyed the view outside.

Nakul belonged to the family of Prime Celestials. It was believed that the big bang was created as a result of their amusement and a whole different world was formed. Prime Celestials were part of the universal system; their every action caused the creation and destruction of the worlds, planets and galaxies. They were the reason why the universe worked the way it did.

They all worshiped the energy called 'Supreme Celestials'. The energy that gave birth to the first Prime Celestial that further lead to many more generations of other celestial beings. The all-powerful prime celestials acted upon the will of the Supreme Celestial. It was untamed energy, the energy that could control all the Prime Celestials, their wills, their actions, and their future. There were three Supreme Celestials. One looked after the creation, another looked after the upkeep of the creation and the last one's role was destruction and to re-create everything, keeping the cycle of life going. Nakul's father was the highest ranked Prime Celestial, and as a result, he was rewarded with a son that had the fragments of all the three Supreme Celestials in him.

A being with powers of infinite energy who would know no boundaries. All the three supreme celestials gave a part of their energy to him. Not just as a reward but to store their energies somewhere, just in case the world needed it in their absence.

His creations would lead to destructions and that would lead to balance. The kid was given powers which knew no end. Nakul's mother thought it was a boon, but he was gifted these powers to take care of the universe. He didn't know the repercussions of his actions and it had to be kept a secret. At a very young age, he was sent to a planet where there was no way he could realize his true powers and where he could bring about a change, knowingly or unknowingly.

The supreme celestial himself dropped him on the planet called 'Phruthvi' -a planet that he would look after, unknowingly.

Nakul's eyes stopped glowing; he saw something that scared him.

"What! You! How did you do that?" he asked Kison as he moved away from him.

"Does that answer the question of how I will be able to stop you? Stop involving your powers into things that would lead to no good. Nakul, we expect more from you," Kison said.

Back to the rink.

Nakul fell down on his knees as he was exhausted.

He looked at Yudhraj, who was standing close to him and dropped down on the floor.

"I am definitely gonna need some strong stuff now," he mumbled and he passed out.

Chapter 16

The game of dice

Kison looked at Yudhraj who was standing next to him and said, "I think, it's better if you take everyone back to the ship. I have asked a couple of men to help you."

"Alright!" Yudhraj said as he tried to pick Nakul up by putting a hand around his shoulder, Arjun did the same and they both dragged him out of the field.

"The battle has ended! Everyone evacuate this place now," Kison announced.

Everyone heard him and started to leave silently.

Virakanna left the place too.

In the king's private room.

Kison, Sage Vyaan, Dronaji, Bhishmaji and his five sons stood inside the room uncomfortably.

"What was all that?" King Duta questioned Kison, who was standing in front of him.

"My King! I have absolutely no idea; I didn't know something like this will happen in the middle of the combat," Kison replied.

Diyohan aggressively approached him and said, "You are a liar. Don't you say you weren't aware that one of them is a mystic? If you had to bring in mystics, you could have told us. We have a fair amount of them with us too."

"Relax Diyohan, I repeat I didn't know," Kison said without looking at him as he looked at Virakanna who was still terrified with what had happened. He leaned on a nearby wall and was quietly trying to comprehend the battle.

Dushalya finally decided to speak what he felt; he had been silently observing everything since the coronation ceremony. He came forward and said, "With all due respect Kison, I do not appreciate you trying to bring our brother down by pulling such tricks. Challenging the throne is an insult and coming from you, it hurts our sentiments, but I will not let emotions come in between. A mystic? You let a mystic fight my brother? He killed one of us! Just because he was a clone doesn't mean it doesn't matter to us, we will mourn his death and avenge our fallen brother."

"You have every right to be angry, but now the challenge has been accepted and nobody can back out. As you know, they are not just simple men. I don't know what was happening to Bheem before he was knocked unconscious or how Nakul turned out to be a mystic, but I think we all should defeat them with our brains," Kison said as he looked at Bhishmaji.

"Don't look at me! I do as my King asks me to! If he asks me to rip apart the mystic I will do that too," he replied.

"LIES! AGAIN LIES!" Diyohan screamed.

"At first, you challenge us on behalf of them and now you want us to defeat them? What kind of games are you playing with us?" he asked Kison.

"I may have challenged you, but my loyalty still lies with King Duta and the kingdom. On being the chief advisor of the King, it is not only my responsibility to choose a perfect heir for him but also help his sons win a battle no matter how slim the chances are," Kison said with a smile.

"What? Slim chances? How dare you?" Diyohan yelled and approached Kison.

Dushalya stopped him and said, "Kison! I am personally disappointed with your actions. How can you not have confidence in Diyohan when you have seen him for so long, you have seen him win battles, you have seen him fight wild animals with his bare hands. You have also seen him plan strategies that have destroyed entire armies."

Kison looked at Dushalya and said, "I don't owe you an explanation but go and ask the people of the kingdom if they love your brother or fear him. Everything you said above had a negative connotation. Has he done anything that has spread joy amongst people? No, don't beat yourself!

"A true leader is not the one who is strong but the one who makes his followers feel the strongest."

"Your father is blind and yet everyone in the kingdom

is happy. With the help of your uncle Vidurm, he has conquered the world. Winning battle requires killing, but it has to stop after a point. It's not like your brother doesn't know this, but he doesn't want to stop," Kison added.

There was a pin drop silence in the room, a silence of acceptance.

Sage Vyaan cleared his throat and said, "Okay! How do we win this challenge?"

Kison left a sigh and said, "We will think of a way to do that."

"But I think we should take a break and let the Princes get ready," he added.

"Get ready? I say let's use the card of hell on these men! Father, we can call up creatures from the under-world that will finish these men. Not just that, we know people who are cannibals and ruthless murderers. Let's use them and finish these five men even before this starts again...." Diyohan said but was interrupted by someone.

"Or else beat them with our brains?" Dushalya said.

"How?" Intrigued by his brother's opinion, Diyohan asked.

"There is nothing as a fair fight and with such enemies against us, let's not even be fair," he replied.

"So what's your plan?" Diyohan asked.

"Let's play a gamble with them! Let's use the dice of

Shakun Mama against them and win the game even before they understand, how about that?" Dushalya replied.

"Sounds great!" Diyohan said.

"So it's settled then! Let's send them an invitation for a game and end this nonsense!" Dushalya said and looked at Kison.

"Dice of Shakun is meant to show results the way you wish them to, isn't that cheating again?" Kison asked.

"You should be the last person to hold the torch of fair play Kison. Clearly, they are not ordinary men and Shakun mama's dice is a better idea than what Diyohan has in his mind," Dushalya said.

"Okay then! Whatever you think is right! I am in full favor of what the King decides," Kison replied and looked at the King.

After a brief silence, the King left a sigh and said, "Hmmm! I think this is fine. Send them this message. Set the table in the centre of the royal court and let's roll the dice exactly seven days from today."

Chapter 17
Seeds of Shanti.

The 30th Century was not just the era of advanced technology but an era where Ayurveda took a whole different turn. The government passed the 'Drug Legalization Motion' and the face of illness changed forever. As the name suggests, the government gave a green signal to the usage of drugs that were derived from Nature. It resulted in medical advancement and the law and order became efficient. The usage of recreational drugs wasn't legalized overnight; it took several years of failure until one man gave up everything to turn this thought into a reality. Dr. Anurag Sinha was the person who played a key role in making this happen. He contributed all his life earnings into the study of drugs and its effects. He not only worked on his research, but also provided funds for students who wanted to get into this study and didn't have proper funding. Anurag was arrested several times for standing against the government. Dr. Sinha was 30 years old when he presented his thesis. The argument was so strong that the government finally passed the Drug Legalize Motion. Dr. Sinha was a young and passionate guy, he didn't have a doctorate yet people referred to him as 'Doctor.'

He was a student of Arts and studied Human Nature.

Born in a trader's family, he quickly picked up the traits of being good at business. He started working over the motion when he was 16. Being part of illegal rallies, meetups, attacks on the government offices, supplying drugs to the people who needed a cure.

After the motion was passed, the biggest roadblock was how to centralize the entire trade. Thousands of growers and peddlers came out and started selling drugs. That gave rise to the spiked drug usage, harmful drugs and illegal substances. That's when Dr. Sinha saved the day again; he made a deal with the government to monopolize the creation and selling of the recreational drugs and thus he formed his company 'Seeds Of Shanti Corp'. This deal with the government gave rights only to Seeds Of Shanti to produce and sell drugs. A small idea turned out to bring a paradigm shift in the entire world's economy. Seeds Of Shanti not only focused on the sale of drugs, but also got into the natural form of medicines and Vaccines. Medicines that wiped out the entire pharmaceutical industry in a matter of just a few years. Sinha had no competition; he had his monopoly over the whole globe. For him, it was easier as his raw material was available in abundance in nature.

Years later, he also started dealing on the intergalactic level; he was known across the galaxies for his medicines. A man with so much light was bound to burn in that same light. Fifteen years later he was the richest man on the planet. He was truly living the best of his life.

He, along with this wife, was standing in the balcony of a house that had a beach in its backyard. It was a private beach; nobody could enter the location, the sky was clear of the stars, no hovering vehicles or any advertising holograms were present. He looked outside, took a big drag from his joint, and passed it to his wife, who was standing next to him.

"We have achieved everything, haven't we?" he said.

His wife puffed some smoke and passed it back to him, "It was all in your destiny, honey," she said as she looked at the moon. The moon was shattered into pieces, the human greed to expand the real estate made corporates start construction on the moon, little did they know. The moon wasn't a place for humans, it couldn't take the continuous drilling, and finally, a huge explosion shattered the entire moon across space. The broken moon just hovered in the place where it was supposed to be.

"I want to tell you something, something I have been hiding from you for years," he said as he threw his joint in the waste bin.

"Yes? What is it?" She asked curiously.

"Before I start, I owe you an apology and I want to tell you that I love you and our kid more than anything else," he said as he looked at their son playing with a robot inside the room.

"Hey, what happened? What did you do?" She asked, worried to learn the truth.

"Do you remember when I went for the Drug conference in Greater Delhi a year after our marriage?"

She took a while to recollect and said, "Yes, I guess I remember that."

"While I was there… I got close to a woman," he said as he hung his head in shame

"What? And then what happened?"

"A few years ago she got in touch with me and told me that she gave birth to a son and that he was mine," his voice lowered.

"How could you do this to me?" she asked as she was filled with rage.

"I am sorry! It was a huge day for us. My drugs took me out on a ride and this is what happened"

"What about the child now?"

"She gave birth to a boy, her economic condition was not good, so I paid her ten crore rupees and asked her to enrol the kid in F.A.T.E," he said.

"And?" she inquired.

"I am going to the academy to see the kid for the first time tomorrow. He is my eldest son," he said as he walked inside.

"How can anyone just get into F.A.T.E.? They need special skill sets, don't they?" she inquired as she followed him.

"I paid them a little and asked them to tell him that he was found on the streets and was an orphan," Sinha said as he looked at his son.

His wife looked at their son and said, "Arjun, let's go to sleep!"

"Are you going to leave me?" he asked her.

"I am leaving tomorrow morning. Need some time alone, I am taking Arjun with me," she replied as she lay on the bed.

Anurag didn't say anything and lay beside her.

Arjun was 12 years old. He lived a life which most of the people could only dream of, but that made him unaware of the surroundings. He didn't know how the outside world was. Whatever he saw was a part of the entertainment, that was his life.

Anurag couldn't sleep; he slid a finger in the air, pointing towards the ceiling. It displayed 3:34 pm on the flat surface. He left a sigh and waved at the ceiling and the digits disappeared.

He suddenly heard the door opening.

He didn't move but quietly pulled his iron wrist band towards him; it was a slim iron band which had biometric on it and had a small red light that blinked. As soon as he wore it, the red light turned to green. He clenched his fist and nanoparticles came out of the band. Pointy sharp iron knuckles were formed over his hand.

He quickly jumped out of his bed to punch the person who entered the room, but he suddenly stopped. That person pointed an electro-wave blaster towards Arjun who was fast asleep.

"You move and his head turns into dust," the man said.

It was dark and Anurag couldn't see who it was. He struggled to get a glimpse of his face.

"Who are you?"

Anurag tried to clench his fist again, but before he could, the man pressed a button, and his blaster made a buzzing noise.

"No! No! No, wait," he screamed.

His scream was loud enough for Arjun and his wife to wake up.

"Good! Now that everyone is up, let's begin the party," the man said and hit Anurag's face with the gun. He fell unconscious on the floor with a loud thud.

Anurag woke up and found himself tied to a chair and next to him was his wife.

"What's happening?" she asked.

Anurag had suffered a concussion, but he looked around frantically for his son. He noticed that Arjun was sitting on a chair looking at them and behind him stood the man.

"Who the hell are you?" Anurag yelled at him

The man ignored what Anurag said.

"Hey kid, I am giving you two options right now!" Arjun looked back at the person with helpless eyes.

"Your parents are sitting in front of you. I am going to kill both of them," he said in a very cold voice.

"What? He is just a child. What the hell is wrong with you?" his mother yelled.

"Shut up," the person yelled back at her.

He patted Arjun's head and said, "You have to kill one of them to keep the other one alive," and handed a laser gun in his hand.

"What is wrong with you, you psychopath?" Anurag screamed at the man.

"Guards! Guards! Guards!" Anurag screamed as loud as he could.

"Oh! I killed all of them. So it's just us here now," the person replied.

"What do you want from us?" Anurag asked him as his voice cracked.

He didn't pay attention and looked at Arjun.

"So! Who is your favourite parent?" the man asked.

Arjun was scared as he held the gun in his trembling hands and he started crying.

"Oh, what a cry baby," the person said as he clocked his blaster and pointed it towards his father.

"NO!" Arjun screamed.

"Kill me!" his mother yelled

Anurag looked at her with tears in his eyes.

"Please forgive me..." he whispered.

Arjun stood up and looked at the person and said, "Please leave us!"

"If you don't kill either of them! I will kill both your parents! You decide if you want to live with one parent or be an orphan," as he pressed a button on the blaster and the barrel of the blaster widened up.

"No, wait. Please wait," he begged the person.

"I think you don't want either of them," he replied.

Arjun cried even louder.

"Choose one! Either your treacherous father or your helpless mother and be quick. You have five seconds," he said as he pointed his blaster towards them.

Arjun didn't know what to do.

"Five, four..." he started the count down.

Arjun pulled up the gun with no idea what to do.

"Three, two..." he kept the countdown going.

"One... Alright then both of them shall die," he said as he was about the pull the trigger.

Arjun fired the gun.

He shot his father in his stomach and dropped the gun on the ground.

"NO!!" his mother yelled out.

Arjun never faced any challenges in his life. His father had been away most of the time and he lived with his mother in the world's most lavish house. Arjun lacked common sense as everything came to him easily. He didn't know what to do when. A situation like this stopped the understanding of the real and put him in a state he never thought he would be in.

"Good call, kid," the person said as he looked at Arjun who dropped on his knees.

"Now your mother dies!" he said as he pointed the blaster towards her, pressed a button and the barrel became thin. He then pulled the trigger. The blaster emitted waves that crushed her body and turned it into dust.

Due to the force, Anurag fell off his chair, bleeding and choking on his own blood.

"NO!" Arjun yelled his lungs out as he saw this!

"Okay then! This was for my wife with whom you slept, 16 years ago," he said as he looked at Anurag who was chocking on his own blood.

"Now! I am gonna take your son away from you, just the way you took mine and he has to live a miserable life," he said as he pulled Arjun and started walking out.

"Oh and just to clear the tracks...." He said as he threw a small cube near Anurag.

It kept on beeping.

He dragged a howling Arjun as he moved away from the destruction.

Anurag struggled to move away from the beeping cube. It beeped faster and finally exploded.

The man took Arjun towards the sea.

"Now you little piece of shit, you will have to live a life

without your parents and rot in hell," he said as he threw Arjun in a skiff.

He got in the skiff and entered the coordinates of a place.

"Destination locked," the machine said.

The motor started buzzing.

The man jumped out of the skiff and pointed his blaster towards himself.

"You are a curse," he said to Arjun and blew his own face.

The motor started and automatically drove off from there. Arjun was terrified to see this. And he sat on the floor crying and shivering in shock.

Chapter 18

Kid from the street

The skiff finally stopped near a dock. Arjun got up to see where he reached and he was confused to find himself in a strange place. There were hundreds of cargo ships being loaded and unloaded, the entire place was in chaos and everyone was shouting on top of each other.

He was scared and still in shock. He got off the skiff and started walking. He walked towards a man and asked, "Excuse me, sir, where am I?"

"You don't know? What are you doing here?" the man asked.

"Sir, can you take me to the nearest Seeds of Shanti office?"

As soon he said the words 'seeds of shanti'- everyone stopped where they were and stared at him.

Young Arjun was confused to see this.

"Why do you wanna go to the shit hole?" A person asked.

"Well, it's my father's company. This place is new and I don't know where else to go," he said as he looked around.

"Oh! So, you are the son of that prick?" the same person inquired as he approached Arjun.

Arjun moved a few steps backward as he was scared to see the men.

Another person came from behind and said, "We all lost our jobs because of your father. His greed and politics ruined the lives of hundreds of us."

"Kill him," a man yelled from behind.

And a mob of ten-fifteen people started hitting him, within few seconds he was on the ground and everyone continued to kick him. Arjun yelled and screamed for mercy, but the loss of the people was bigger than the cry for mercy of a little boy.

Everyone stopped after a while and looked at Arjun who was on the ground; he was motionless, his clothes were covered in dirt and foot imprints. He was bleeding terribly. Everybody left from there, while leaving a person spat on his face. A boy who was born with a silver spoon in his mouth had to taste dirt today. Feelings like sorrow, pain and stress were farfetched for him. He was losing his consciousness as he looked around for help; he tried to get up with all the strength he had but collapsed on the ground and passed out.

He finally woke up after a while; he had blurry vision and couldn't understand where he was. He looked at his right side and saw a girl sitting next to him on the chair nearby. Arjun couldn't see properly, but she looked like someone who was in her early twenties. She was wearing a ripped tank top and a pajama which was patched at many places. She looked tired; her hair was messy and tangled like they weren't washed for a couple of days.

She was chewing gum and making weird faces as if the gum were too sticky.

Arjun tried to get up.

"Hey, Kid! Relax. You are in no state to even move," she said and Arjun could see the bright pink gum stuck to her teeth.

"Who...Who are you?" he asked.

"My name is Kara; I found you on the streets two days ago."

"Two days? I have been sleeping for two days?" he asked as he saw the bandages that covered his body.

"Unconscious is the right word. I found you in a very terrible state. I picked you up and brought you here. Heard they bashed you because you are the son of Mr. Sinha, yeah?" she asked as she opened a small box and pulled out a pill.

"Yes! Are you going to hit me too?" Arjun innocently asked with a shaking voice.

"No, kid! Relax! I ain't gonna do anything like that. Your dad has provided some good quality strains in the market. The hospitals have used them so well, someone I knew cured his cancer because of your dad's subsidized meds for underprivileged population," she said as she passed the tablet to him.

He held it in his hands and asked, "What is this?"

"Chill! It's a pain killer. You are probably gonna take

some time to get back on your feet. Till then be my guest. You won't get luxury here, but you will survive."

Something beeped on the table next to the bed. It was a small transparent slate. She immediately picked it up and it projected a hologram.

'1 new task.'

She touched the envelope icon.

'New cleaning duty at Dock no.4.'

'Accept or deny?'

She selected 'Accept.'

'Reporting time: estimate 20 mins'

And the hologram went off.

"What do you do exactly?" Arjun asked

"I clean the docks, I am one of the cleaning guys out there," she said as she picked up her trench coat which had an emblem on the right side and "ON DUTY" written on the back of the coat.

"I gotta go! I will be back in a couple of hours. Please rest, don't move. The water is on your left side. Not from the purifier but it won't give you a bad stomach," she said and she moved away.

Arjun looked around; the room wasn't in a good state. There were several cracks on the walls and it looked like the roof could fall anytime. There was a small broken window from where he could hear the ships and flying cargo jets. He didn't care about the room, he wanted to get well at the earliest and he closed his eyes to relax and fell asleep.

As months passed, Kara and Arjun bonded well. Kara took good care of him and tried to provide him with good food and shelter. Arjun was pleased to have a person like her around after the tragedy of losing both his parents. Kara took care of him like an elder sister. Sometimes she took him with her for cleaning duties and earned an extra buck, that night they would eat luxury food. Arjun knew he was at a safe place, nothing could fill in the loss of his parents, but atleast he knew that the feeling of love and care will not be missing.

One day both of them were returning from their cleaning duties and Kara asked.

"Hey kid, don't you think we should visit the headquarters of your dad's office? It's been five months now. I am sure he must have made some will or something like that for you, don't you think?"

"No sister! I don't want to go there. The headquarters reminds me of my dad. I don't want the money; I am fine this way. I am happy with you," he said as they walked down the alley.

"Ah! no kid, it's not about the money. I am not sure for how long I can provide you with good food. I barely make something. It's for you; you might live a better life if there is some provision out there," she said as she ran her fingers through Arjun's hair.

"Makes sense, okay. We can go there and check. How far is the headquarters from here?" he asked

"Well, it's in Greater Mumbai, it takes around 5 hours to reach there. If we take a sonic jet, we will reach in 3 hours. If not it might take us more, but unfortunately we don't have enough money for the sonic jet. So we will have to travel via cargo ship only," she said as they reached the house.

"Sister, thank you for everything. I don't know how I would repay you," he said and his eyes were moist.

"Come on, you are a good kid. Besides that, we are a family, right? If this goes well, you will take me out to those expensive sky shopping malls. Deal?" she said as she opened the door.

"DEAL," Arjun said playfully.

The next morning...

Kara had to pull some strings to get into the cargo ship. After 6 hours of sea route journey, they reached Greater Mumbai II dock. As soon as they got down, they could see a huge glass building which was located far away. It shined bright and was the tallest of all the huge buildings. On top of the building, there was a huge symbol of Seeds Of Shanti.

"There's your palace, my Prince," Kara said in a dramatic manner to Arjun.

They both walked till the entrance of the headquarters.

The security guard instantly stopped them!

"Hey you junkies, buzz off!" He said rudely.

Both of them weren't dressed in their finest attire; their clothes were dirty and torn in many places.

Kara approached the guard with anger and said, "Aye! Do you even know who you are talking to? Look at him," and she pointed her finger towards Arjun.

The guard looked at him and exclaimed, "HOLY SHIT, this can't be true."

He immediately touched his coms and said, "Boss! You might want to come to Gate A. You are not going to believe this."

The head of security came, and he was shocked too.

"What the hell, master Arjun? We all thought you died in the fire," he said.

Both of them were later taken to the board room where they waited for all the other directors to come.

"Kid listen up! Do not tell them the part where you shot your father, okay? You do that, and they will charge you for murder. Do you get me?" she asked in a very firm voice.

Arjun was very overwhelmed; that place reminded him of this dad and the horrors of that night!

Everyone came in the room and Arjun told them what happened, just another version of it.

After a brief discussion, it was decided that Arjun gets all the shares of his dad and the accounts department would help him to retain all the wealth of his parents.

"So, congratulations, master Arjun. You are probably the youngest billionaire alive. Leave alone the assets. Until you don't become an adult, we will help you out with everything," one of the directors said.

"I have one condition," Arjun promptly said.

"What condition?" one of the directors asked.

"I want all the money and assets to be equally divided between Kara sister and me."

Kara was shocked to hear this.

"That's a huge amount of money we are talking about master Arjun, we can't do that," a director interrupted.

"Please, I want to do this and then only we can go ahead," Arjun replied, rather immaturely.

He did what his heart felt was right.

"Alright! We will work on this and see to it that we divide the wealth equally," another director said. His voice was heavy and determined.

"Thank you, Uncle Singh, this means a lot," Arjun said with a wide smile.

Arjun along with Kara, were escorted to the nearest guest house and were given lavish amenities to enjoy.

IN THE BOARD ROOM.

Mr. Singh was looking outside his glass window where he could see the entire city.

"Mr. Singh! Why did you commit such a thing to Master Arjun?" one of the directors asked him.

"Calm Down! I am not letting all that wealth go to some roadside cleaner. If the money stays with Arjun, it's in the company for the next few years. I said that to make him believe there is a way."

"So what do we do now?" the director asked Mr. Singh.

"Kill her, if she doesn't live, there won't be any division," he said and looked outside again.

Chapter 19

Drupa

Next morning the five of them gathered in the assembly hall of the ship. As everyone spent their time in the healing pods, they were back to normal and hydrated.

Nakul had a heavy head as he looked around and said, "Man! the lights are damn bright, can we please dim them?"

The ship replied, "Good morning Nakul, but the lights are dim and it's the natural lighting that is coming inside. Should I shut the window flaps?"

"Never mind," he said softly.

Bheem walked in, looking much better.

"What happened to me?" he asked Yudhraj

"You were poisoned, with some kind of plant venom."

"How is that possible? The poisons don't work on me if you remember."

Deva pressed a few keys and from the center of the table, a hologram popped out.

"So, it wasn't a deadly poison; its main purpose was to paralyze someone temporarily. I don't think you are immune to that," Deva said as the report was shown on the hologram.

"Hmm, makes sense," Bheem replied as he looked at the reports.

Yudhraj, who was sitting next to Deva, said, "Okay, the things didn't go the way we planned. Firstly the attack on Bheem and then Kison intervening in the battle to stop Nakul."

"What exactly happened, Nakul? Both of you froze for a while. How could he even stop you?" Yudhraj inquired.

Nakul cleared his throat and said, "Look, man, it was pretty intense. Trust me this Kison guy is not normal, he was in the astral plane with me and he controlled it too. Can you believe that?"

Deva looked at Nakul and said, "The way he suddenly appeared in the field and stopped your punch explains a lot."

Arjun broke his silence as he heard all of them talking amongst themselves, "I think we all have to be prepared for anything that comes up. I am sure they are not going to be okay with the kind of embarrassment they all faced. I am wondering what is coming up next."

The screen chimed and it showed Kison walking towards the ship.

"And here he is," Deva said.

Kison came inside the ship and stood in front of them.

"Hope you all are doing fine?" Kison asked and looked at Nakul.

"Man! Don't even look at me. You are damn scary and creepy bro," Nakul said as he covered his eyes with his palms.

Arjun got up from his seat as he looked at Kison, "Whatever you did out there was impressive, but this duel didn't finish. So either we finish it or go back. You got any news for us?"

"Yes, of course, I have and that is why I am here," Kison replied.

"1 Rupee bet, this is going to be bad news," Nakul said and he still had his eyes covered.

"Not exactly bad news. Given the circumstances, the King wants you to play a board game with his son."

"What are we? Kids?" Yudhraj asked in a very irritated tone.

"No! This is more like a life and death board game, a gamble. Anyone of you can play it and on the other side it's going to be Diyohan," Kison said, and he looked around.

"What are you looking for?" Deva asked out of curiosity.

"Is there anything with you? I need to draw and explain. Like coal or something?" Kison asked,

"It's quite primitive for us; we have holographic sketchbooks. You want to try?" Deva asked as he started pressing a few keys.

"No, let it be! I will explain it verbally."

Everyone looked at Kison as he was about to start.

"There are going to be two players, sitting across a table. A small board will be placed in between; one by one, each one has to roll the dice. The dice will have numbers on all the six sides and the board will have equal number of squares on it. The pebble has to be moved accordingly, but in between, there will be a green block, each time anybody's pebble reaches the green block, he can ask his opponent to do whatever he wishes too, no killing will be involved, but he will surely want to embarrass you," Kison finished explaining the game.

"Are you clear?" he asked

Nakul was scratching his head as he was trying to figure out what all Kison said, while his other hand covered his eyes.

"I figured it out. It seems doable," Yudhraj said.

Arjun looked at him and said, "It seems fair too, given the fact that it's all part of luck."

"Right! I will do it," Yudhraj said as he looked at Kison.

"Okay then! The gamble is in six days" Kison replied as he turned his back towards them and walked away.

Deva quickly got up and went towards Kison; he heard Deva's footsteps approaching and turned back.

"Yes?" Kison instantly turned around as he was expecting Deva to come and talk to him.

"Any tips?" Deva inquired.

"Well, hope for the best. Remember, hope is the strongest weapon in your arsenal; make sure you never run out of it," Kison replied as he emphasized on the word hope and smiled in his remarkable way.

"Oh, by the way, you might want to take a tour of the city. There is a nice handicraft fair going on today. But see to it that you go in disguise, people have gone crazy and a lot of them want to meet you," he added

Kison then walked towards the door, it automatically opened and he walked out. The door hissed shut.

"Did he leave? Can I open my eyes now?" Nakul asked.

Bheem looked at him and said, "What? You had your eyes covered the entire time?"

"Yeah man! That dude's scary, he reminds me of all the strict teachers I had in the academy," and he finally opened his eyes.

Deva giggled and said, "Okay then, let's go and visit the city. Let's explore the culture. Alright?"

Nakul took a deep breath and said, "Yeah in those uncomfortable clothes."

Everyone got up and went to their respective rooms, changed and regrouped in the hall.

They left the ship and went walking towards the city. It was so festive out there; it looked like everyone had something to put on display.

Some sold animals, while some sold crockery, while others had games that involved bow and arrow shooting.

The bow and arrow game intrigued Arjun as he walked

towards the stall. The stall had a lot of people gathered there. Arjun and Yudhraj made their way through the crowd and saw that there was a lady standing with a wooden bow in her hand. Many mud balls were kept on the table and behind it, there was a wooden plank.

She was a fine lady, long black hair which were tied behind her head; she was fair and tall. Her attire was different from other women present at the fair. A combination of red and peacock blue that had aesthetic golden design across the borders. Unlike others, she wasn't wearing heavy jewellery. Her toned muscles set her apart and made it evident that she knew how to fight. She wore a simple necklace, but that was enough to enhance her beauty. Her lips and pink cheeks just made her look even more beautiful. She shot the arrows while she was blindfolded.

"Alright! Who's next?" she asked.

"I am," a man walked and picked up one ball in his hand.

"Ready?" he asked.

"Always!" she replied with a lot of enthusiasm as she placed an arrow over her bow.

And the man threw the ball towards the other end of the stall. She pulled back her arrow and shot it.

The arrow pierced through the mud ball within a split second.

The crowd went wild.

"Nice!" Yudhraj exclaimed

"Impressive" Arjun said in a soft tone.

"I am sure you can do this too, right, Arjun?" Yudhraj said as he looked at Arjun.

"Of course, man! "Arjun replied and he smirked.

As the crowd kept on cheering, she opened her blindfold. As she pulled the cloth away, her hair slipped open and black shiny, silky hair fell on her face. She shook her head and looked around. Her eyes were blue and the smudged kohl made them look like they had deep secrets.

"Thank you, thank you!" she exclaimed.

"So? Who's next?" she asked as she looked at the crowd.

Yudhraj came forward and said, "Let me throw them!"

"Oh! Look at you! Alright. Let's do this," she said as she blindfolded herself again.

Yudhraj swung his hand in the air, stretched his wrist, and threw the ball. As soon as he threw it, she shot the arrow, the arrow went towards the ball at a great speed, but before the arrow could hit the ball, it changed its direction and inclined towards the left side. She missed it.

The arrow hit the wooden plank; she pulled her blindfold away as soon as she heard the sound of an arrow piercing the plank.

"Impossible," she said.

The crowd went silent and left one by one from there.

"How did you do that?" she asked Yudhraj.

"Well, I used my wrist and index finger, I timed to loop the rotation in the air to flick it considering the weight of the ball, so the ball went straight but deviated from its original path due to the loop and went sideways," he replied

"Spin!" she exclaimed.

"Yes! That's right! "

"Smart! Very smart!" she said as she kept her bow on the table.

"What is your name?" Yudhraj asked as he looked at her pretty eyes.

"Drupa," she replied and folded the cloth and kept it on the table.

Yudhraj was mesmerized by her beauty and the way she shot those arrows earlier.

"What's your name? I have never seen you before. You aren't from around?"

"Ah, no! We …we are not from around. We stay in the nearby sector," he stammered

"Sector? What is that?" she asked as she heard that word for the first time.

"I mean, village. Nearby village. We came here to visit the fair," Yudhraj said as he looked around.

"Okay. Good then! Hope you have a good time here! There are going to be a board games in a few days between the prince and some guy who apparently is the leader of 4 outsiders. Did you see the duel that happened the other day?" she asked him.

"Oh no, I just heard of it. We are also going to stay here long enough to watch the board game," he replied, trying to not get into the details.

"Okay then, I got to go. See you around," she said and left.

Yudhraj stood there even after she left, looking at her disappear into the crowd.

Arjun came near him and said "Focus, you got a big game to play."

"Yes, I remember," he replied as he kept looking for her in the crowd.

"She is beautiful," Yudhraj said with a smile.

Chapter 20
Let's Roll the Dice

It was game day and everyone had gathered to watch the epic gamble. Yudhraj sat on the chair and looked at the board game. Diyohan sat in front of him.

They both looked into each other's eye, Diyohan knew the game and Yudhraj knew that he had to win this. He had made up his mind; he believed that the first attack should be strong enough to shake the roots of the opponent; he decided to go heavyweight from the beginning.

He looked around and noticed the number of people who came to witness the gamble.

Drupa was present there too, she looked at Yudhraj sitting on the chair, and she was shocked.

"Hey, it's the spin guy!" she said to herself.

"Hey! Yudhraj!" she yelled and waved at him

He instantly turned towards her and waved back. She wore a beautiful pink saree, he couldn't control his smile and blushed.

"All the best!" she yelled with a big smile.

Diyohan noticed this and smirked as evil plans rose in his mind.

"Ready to lose?" Diyohan asked Yudhraj as he picked up the dice and handed it over to him.

"Too early to predict the end results, my friend," Yudhraj said as he held the dice in his hand.

He tossed the dice and it landed on the number '5'.

He moved his pebble five blocks from the starting point.

Diyohan picked up the dice and tossed it on the board, the number that appeared was '2'.

Diyohan moved the pebble and it was just one block short from reaching the green zone.

"Missed by an inch, looks like you got a little lucky here," Diyohan said.

Yudhraj didn't react; he picked up the dice as he gathered his positive thoughts at one place as he wished for something good to happen in the next move; he then tossed it on the board.

The number that appeared was '4'.

Yudhraj moved his pebble, and it stopped on a green block.

"No!" Diyohan exclaimed and looked at his brothers.

"This is not good," Dushan asked Dushalya who was twisting his moustache.

"Pure luck? Or did he really wished before tossing it?" Dushan questioned again.

"That's not important anymore; I am just waiting for what he is going to ask," Dushalya replied

Yudhraj raised his hand up in the air and dramatically said, "I want half of your kingdom."

The entire crowd went silent.

"What the hell, no! You aren't even getting a tiny part of it," Diyohan exclaimed.

Arjun who was standing at a distance, smiled and said, "Hmm! Classic Yudhraj, strong-arming at the very beginning."

Yudhraj looked at Diyohan and said, "Rules are rules! I want half of it, or declare that you got scared and end this now."

The King who sat on his throne heard this. As usual, Kison stood next to him.

"Kison, did you tell them about the secret?" he asked Kison.

"No my King, my loyalty is towards you! I didn't tell them how to use the dice."

Diyohan laughed as he heard Yudhraj.

"Scared? And me? I am the mighty Prince. I will give you half of the kingdom. Enjoy!" Diyohan said as he banged his fist on the board.

"Good! Accepting your defeat is a sign of a true warrior, let's continue," Yudhraj said in a very sarcastic tone.

Diyohan picked up the dice and rolled it on the board, but this time his pebble reached the green block.

"I want you to go and punch the old lady that is standing on your right. Punch as hard as you can," Diyohan said and laughed in a wicked manner.

"What? Are you out of your mind? I am not doing this," Yudhraj said in a firm voice.

"Rules are rules," Diyohan said imitating Yudhraj.

"Not doing it at all," Yudhraj screamed and looked at the old lady on his right, she looked fragile, she was leaning on a stick for support.

"If you don't do it. I will. I am sure you punch like a little girl. Your punch won't make any difference, but mine will kill her! Choose for yourself," Diyohan said as he looked at the old lady.

Nakul looked at Bheem and said, "Man this prick is so evil. If I am allowed to, I can and I will vaporize him within a second."

Bheem looked back at him and said, "He is bound to lose this game, with these intentions, I don't think he is going to win anything."

Yudhraj left a sigh and got up; he went walking towards the old lady. He looked at her, her eyes were moist, and she was shivering out of fear.

Yudhraj clenched his fist and landed a punch on her shoulder. She fell, and everyone gasped. He quickly rushed to pick her up.

He dropped on his knees and held her.

"I am sorry amma! Please forgive me!" he said as a tear rolled down his eye. She reminded him of the old lady that took care of him while he was still a kid and lived in the orphanage. His sorrow turned into rage and he looked back at Diyohan!

"You monster!" He yelled.

"Oh, come, sit! Let's finish this; there is a lot to come your way," Diyohan replied.

Yudhraj gulped his anger and took his seat once again.

Yudhraj rolled the dice and the number '3' came up. Unfortunately, his pebble couldn't reach the green block.

It was Diyohan's turn; he rolled the dice and number '2' came and it was the green block again. Everyone was scared and were hoping something even more inhuman to happen.

"What now?" Yudhraj asked.

"I want you to do nothing," Diyohan said as he moved from his chair.

"Do nothing?" Yudhraj inquired as he was clueless about what Diyohan was up to.

"Yeah! You will not move or do anything," and he got up from his chair and went walking towards the barricades.

He went near Drupa and pulled her inside.

"What is wrong with you, leave her now!" Yudhraj screamed his head off.

"Don't even try to move, you are going to do nothing!" he said as he grabbed Drupa by her waist.

"Leave me, Prince, please," Drupa cried out loud.

She struggled as Diyohan held her with his strong hands, she managed to push him away and strike him across his face. Diyohan was now angry and he pulled her close to him with a lot of force. She struggled with the strong and ruthless Prince, while he laughed wickedly.

"Leave her, now!" Yudhraj exclaimed, his voice was cracking with his helplessness.

Yudhraj felt a range of emotions as he saw Drupa crying and struggling to break free from Diyohan's grip.

"Somebody stop this!" Yudhraj yelled out, looking at people around.

Nakul took a step ahead but before he could walk any further Arjun stopped him.

"You cannot interfere; nobody can! This is going down bad. We cannot do anything," Arjun said as he placed his hand on Nakul's shoulder.

"But! Look at him, what the hell is he doing?" Nakul said and looked sick.

Drupa pushed him away and tried to escape; she moved a few steps ahead. As she moved, he caught her by her drapes. She lost her balance and fell on the ground. Diyohan pulled her saree such that, it made her roll on the ground. She managed to get up, but Diyohan didn't stop, he kept on pulling the saree. After a point, the entire saree was off her and she was half naked in front of everyone. Diyohan threw the saree away and walked towards her. She was beyond raging by now, her anger knew no limits. Diyohan smiled and caught her from behind restricting her movements. She was helpless, but not powerless. She was ready to do anything that would stop the monster from hurting her anymore. Her hands were numb but her body was burning due to rage. The very next moment, she bit Diyohan's forearm with all her might, such that her teeth penetrated through his thick skin.

Diyohan quickly pushed her away, looked at his wound and sucked his own blood for soothing it. He then looked at her and wickedly smiled.

Drupa was so mad at Diyohan that she no more cared about her clothes, she leaped towards him to punch him.

Diyohan effortlessly caught her by her neck and pinned her down. The force was so massive that it hurt Drupa beyond her understanding.

He put his two fingers under her blouse and looked at Yudhraj.

"Enjoy the view, my friend," he said to a shocked Yudhraj.

He tightened his grip and was about to tear the blouse apart, when suddenly Kison put his arms between them and pulled Diyohan away from her. Drupa crawled away from them, trying to cover her body and looked at the Prince with hateful eyes. In her mind, he wasn't their Prince anymore.

Kison looked at Diyohan and thwacked him in his chest. Kison for the first time lost his composure and hit him hard. Diyohan fell far away from her.

"Enough of this nonsense, how dare you touch a woman without her consent? How dare you do such a heinous act? Shame on you and shame on your blind father, the so-called great King," Kison said as his eyes turned red in rage.

"This is what you have raised?" he asked the Queen. The always proud mother, Queen Gundhi too hung her head in shame.

Kison took off his shawl and wrapped it around Drupa.

Yudhraj ran quickly towards her; she was in a state of shock and cried out loud.

Diyohan got up and looked at Yudhraj.

"I commanded you to do nothing," he yelled from a distance.

Yudhraj looked back at Diyohan in rage and yelled.

"This is it! You don't deserve to live! I challenge you and whatever power you have with you. My team and I will destroy you into bits! I swear to the almighty supreme celestial. I will kill you with my own hands, not only you but your entire family will die, we will slaughter each one of you," said Yudhraj and enraged.

The entire crowd went silent and the sniffs of Drupa echoed around.

The King hung his head in shame and said, "What have you done my child?."

After listening to this, Diyohan charged towards Yudhraj. Before he could reach him, Kison stood in between and said, "Stand down!"

Diyohan controlled his pace as he saw the mighty Kison standing in front of him.

Kison looked at Drupa who wouldn't stop cursing the Prince, he walked near her and said, "Sister, I am sorry this happened to you, sorry I couldn't do anything! Please forgive me and touched her shoulder to help her calm down."

It didn't make Drupa feel any better.

Kison looked at the King, who was sitting on his throne and yelled, "My King! This war will happen, not for the throne but the revenge! Revenge of the injustice that your sons have done, revenge of the killings your sons have done and revenge for harassing an innocent lady. I choose to fight against you. Do whatever you want, bring out whatever devils you have. These men shall defeat them! They are the heroes, Heroes of Wars! And let me tell you, these men alone will finish the entire war and destroy your entire family. My Highness." he said as he stressed on the word Highness.

Yudhraj looked at Kison and felt a sense of confidence.

Arjun, Nakul, Bheem, and Deva walked into the centre and stood beside Yudhraj and stared at Diyohan who stood alone.

Chapter 21

From the Sky

"War? You will die today!" Diyohan yelled as he looked at the five of them!

Yudhraj, who was filled with rage, yelled back, "Let's end this now!"

Rest of the four brothers joined Diyohan.

Dushan was the first one to jump in, he wore his pride, tiger's skin and held an ax in his hand.

Virakanna pulled out two swords and flipped towards his brother.

Dushalya got in with a mace and handed it over to Diyohan. He pulled out his blade ropes quickly.

Yutsu was not the one who would want to get into a fight, but it was the matter of their family's prestige. He had to step in; he reluctantly walked in with a dagger.

Everyone around was thrilled and scared to see the entire scenario. Nobody moved.

Bhishmaji and Dronaji stood right where they were, behind the King.

"Do we join them, my King?" Bhishmaji asked.

"No! My sons are capable of fighting their own wars. Let them."

Nayanraj narrated move by move; he didn't miss even a single action. The King didn't have eyes, but he did not let the King feel the absence of his vision.

Yudhraj looked at the King and spoke loudly, "You have my respect King, but you are not just blinded with sight but with also with love. You cannot see what your son has done, but I apologize now itself, we are not going to spare their lives today."

"May the best win!" the King exclaimed as he raised his hand.

Arjun turned towards Kison and said, "Take Drupa away from here, ask the people to step behind. This is going to get ugly."

"No mercy, use your tech. I will manage everything," Kison said as he looked at the brothers standing in front of him.

He quickly held Drupa and commanded the audience to move behind.

Yudhraj looked at Deva and said, "Can we have the armours? I know they aren't ready but if not now then never."

"Of course, captain!" Deva said as he pulled out the cube from his back pocket and started pressing keys.

Yudhraj impatiently looked at Deva and asked, "How long?"

"Anytime now," Deva replied.

Diyohan was losing his composure and he was filled with rage.

"Come on, let us start this," he exclaimed.

Yudhraj looked at Deva who was almost running out of patience.

"Almost there. Anytime," Deva said as he looked at the cube. The hologram projected a holographic bar which displayed 91%.

Within seconds the percentage bar reached 100% and his device chimed.

A buzzing noise came from above them and the pod that contained their armours landed with a thud. The lids opened up and the armours rapidly flew towards their respective heroes.

Everyone had uniformity running through their armour, it was futuristic, but it had traditional designs that enhanced the aesthetic value of the armour. Each one of them had the symbol of F.A.T.E on their armour that glowed with blue light. The pants were extremely comfortable.

A very high-tech bow was launched towards Arjun, which he caught effortlessly. His armour was white and grey in colour, while combat boots looked ancient that had the same design as that of the others from that era. As soon as the armour was in its place, his right arm illuminated with the bright light.

Bheem's green sleeveless armour adjusted to his huge body, the green and grey shade of the serpent texture was bold and visible even from far. His energy lit mace looked ghastly, as he effortlessly held it in one hand.

Nakul didn't have an armour like others, but his long maroon trench coat with a beautiful golden design, suited him well. His golden boots that extended till his knees looked pretty mesmerizing. He held his spear which had the rare stone at the top.

Yudhraj had a magnificent white cape on his back that made his authority evident. His blue and grey armour with the patches of gold made him stand out from the others. A shield made out of blue light was projected over his left gauntlet and the right gauntlet produced a sabre that was long and sharp.

Deva made sure all the armours were functioning perfectly as he knew they were prototype and that there was a high chance of them malfunctioning. He had to be alert just in case something happens. He wore semi-transparent coloured monocle that covered his left eye and displayed infographics and detailed information about whatever he could see in the frame. His saffron-golden coat wrapped his skinny body. Just like others, his attire too had a traditional design running across the border.

Everyone around was astounded to see this. The primitive men knew nothing about technology, and all of a sudden, they were witnessing something that looked like magic to them.

Virakanna's jaw dropped as he looked at this, "What the hell is this?" he exclaimed.

"Ignore this, their dressing up is not going to change anything," Diyohan said as he charged towards them.

Deva quickly informed them, "All the weapons are not programmed properly, please be ready for some unforeseen incident."

Yudhraj ran towards Diyohan. He approached him with great strength.

His anger was at its peak, Yudhraj couldn't take injustice and the sight he saw, sickened him to his soul. He just wanted to punish Diyohan for what he had done, he channelized his rage into strength and approached Diyohan, a man double his size.

Yudhraj swung his sword with great force, Diyohan blocked it with his mace. The sword hit the mace so hard that sparks were flying. Diyohan felt it too.

Virakanna looked at his brothers and yelled out, "ATTACK!" and all of them charged towards the heroes.

Arjun looked at his teammates and quickly said, "Bheem, you take on Dushan; Nakul, you fight Dushalya; Deva, try and keep up the combat with Yutsu; I will take care of Virakanna! Let's go!"

The royal court turned into a battle zone.

Bheem Vs. Dushan.

Bheem obviously had a better physique than Dushan,

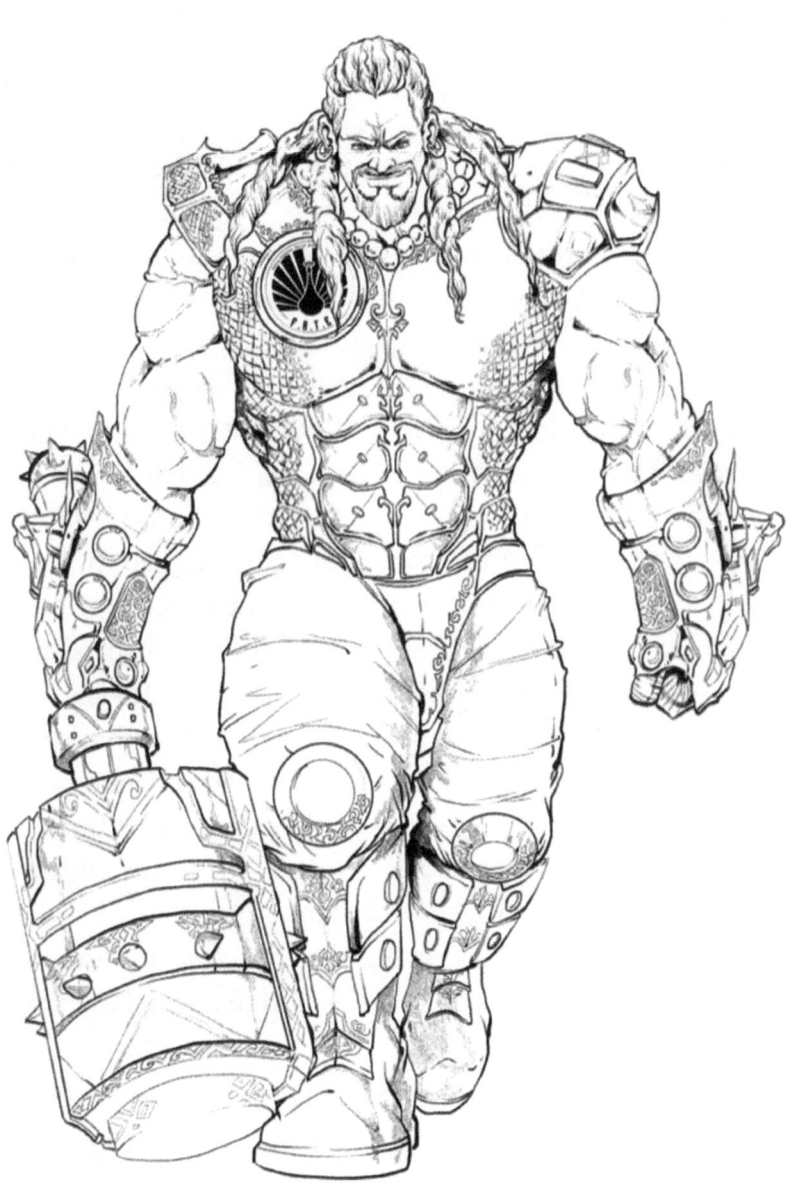

but he was no less, both of them trained to keep their bodies rock solid. Dushan ran towards Bheem with a thick ax in his hand. The tiger skin he wore gave him a sense of pride and strength to fight his opponent. As he flexed, his muscles popped out. His ax was sharp from both sides. He swung his ax towards Bheem's face, Bheem quickly dodged it as he bent backward, sliding down on his knees. The ax moved inches above his nose and he looked up to monitor the attack. Bheem quickly controlled his momentum and got up. Before Dushan could turn around, Bheem hammered him with his mace, the blow was hard; it hit Dushan's face as he turned around to look at Bheem. His ax fell far away, and he instantly dropped down with a thud, bleeding. Bheem didn't miss the opportunity and charged towards him. He jumped towards Dushan, tightened the grip on his mace as he was in the air and prepared to pound him with it. Dushan quickly rolled on his left side and dodged the attack. The blow was so strong that there was a crack on the ground. Bheem pulled back his mace and attacked him again before he could get up. This time he swung his mace from bottom to top and it hit Dushan straight on his face again. Bheem stopped to catch his breath. Dushan was bleeding from his nose and mouth. The damage would have been fatal for a normal man but not for him, he got up and smiled at Bheem.

"That's all you got?" he asked as he wiped the continuously dripping blood from his face.

He ran towards Bheem before Bheem could attack again

he jumped on him and kicked him hard on his face and flipped behind him. It took a few seconds for Bheem to get back to his senses. As he turned around to see, he found Dushan pacing towards him with the ax in his hand. Bheem drew his mace backward and threw it towards Dushan with all his strength. Surprised, Dushan tried to block it with his ax, but as the mace hit the ax, its blade broke. He threw the broken ax away and continued running towards Bheem. Dushan punched him hard. Bheem blocked the punch with his palm, twisted it and turned him around effortlessly. Dushan's back faced Bheem, he twisted it even more and Dushan dropped on his knees. Bheem held his twisted arm and kicked his back. There was a noise of something cracking; it was Dushan's arm. He fell on the ground, grunting and groaning.

Nakul Vs. Dushalya

Nakul stood at his place as Dushalya approached him, twisting his moustache. Dushalya whipped his blade ropes on the ground.

"Are you going to glow again and float in the air?" he asked Nakul.

"Do you want me to? I could wipe out your existence within a second," Nakul said silently.

"Go ahead, do it if you want to," Dushalya said in a calm tone.

"Alright then," Nakul said as he closed his eyes and took a deep breath.

He opened his eyes and saw that Dushalya had rushed towards him. Nakul wasn't levitating, nor was he glowing.

"Damn it! not again," he said to himself as he prepared to swirl his spear.

Dushalya whipped his blade-ropes towards Nakul, the blades happen to hit his coat, but it was strong enough to sustain the attack.

"What happened? No light show today?" Dushalya mockingly asked him.

"I don't need it to beat you, buddy," Nakul replied.

He threw his spear towards Dushalya with great force, He quickly dodged it and whipped his ropes again, one of it gripped around Nakul's forearm. Before Nakul could move, Dushalya pulled Nakul towards him and punched him in his face, Nakul fell on his back. He jumped up quickly before Dushalya could make a move.

"You gotta do better than this," Nakul said as he popped his knuckles.

Dushalya again whipped his ropes, but this time they gripped around Nakul's neck.

He dragged Nakul towards him. Nakul lay on the ground choking and struggling to breathe but in the next moment, Nakul looked at him and giggled.

"What did you think, this is going good for you?" and Nakul laughed out loud.

He held the ropes and pulled Dushalya with a jerk, as he clenched his fist, there was a little light that was produced around his fist. He whisked his fist quickly for the light to go off.

"You are not worth it," Nakul said and pulled Dushalya closer to him.

There was hardly any distance between them, Dushalya reached behind his back and pulled a dagger and quickly tried to stab Nakul in his chest. The blade hit Nakul's coat and broke into pieces.

"Okay, never mind," and Nakul punched him in the face.

Dushalya fell on the ground.

"Did it hurt? Sorry, darling!" Nakul said as he teased Dushalya.

Deva & Yutsu

Yutsu stood in front of Deva and said, "Namastey, I don't want this combat to happen. I don't know you, nor do you know me. We shouldn't be doing this. Look around us; our brothers are bleeding."

Yutsu said as he looked around.

"I am not even into these combats Mr. Yutsu; I am their tech guy. I don't want to fight you either," Deva said as he left a sigh.

Yutsu came closer to him and said, "Is there any way we can stop this?"

"I don't think so."

Yutsu joined his hands and said, "I join my hands and acknowledge the soul inside you. I don't want to hurt the body we have got. May there be peace around."

"Are you adopted?" Deva instantly asked Yutsu, as he was surprised to hear this.

"No! But I have had different thoughts since I was a kid. This is not acceptable," Yutsu replied.

"I did step in with a lot of rage, but I no longer need to be angry at anyone. What my brother did was an utter disgrace and I am ashamed of it."

"Umm! Okay then. We don't have to fight. Let this get over," Deva said as he shook hands with Yutsu.

Diyohan who was fighting with Yudhraj, saw this and yelled, "You stupid prick, keep your policy of non-violence aside and kill him now."

Yutsu joined his hands again and said, "Forgive me, brother, but I cannot do this."

Deva looked at him with a smile and said, "You are a great man, and the world needs more people like you."

Yudhraj Vs. Diyohan

"Stupid Yutsu," Diyohan said as he looked back at Yudhraj.

Yudhraj heard the entire conversation and said, "Wonder how you all turned out to be so evil."

"Keep your mouth shut and fight," Diyohan said as he advanced towards Yudhraj.

Yudhraj swung his sword; Diyohan defended it with his mace again and aimed a punch at Yudhraj's face.

Yudhraj blocked it with his forearm.

Diyohan yelled and banged his head against Yudhraj's face.

It hurt him bad; Yudhraj went a few steps behind but again charged towards him.

He swung his sword and Diyohan swung his mace, they collided, and Yudhraj's sword broke into half.

It did not stop Yudhraj; he attacked him with the broken sword. The edge of the sword cut through the flesh on Diyohan's arm.

"Damn it," Diyohan exclaimed.

He attacked him with his mace, Yudhraj tried to block it with his broken energy sword, but the sword couldn't take the impact and it completely shattered into pieces.

He clenched his fist and attacked Diyohan. Diyohan swung his mace and this time Yudhraj blocked it with his forearm. The shock absorbent shield came in hand. He held the mace and pulled it away with his other hand, he turned around and smashed Diyohan's face with his elbow. Yudhraj quickly clenched his fist again and punched him with an uppercut.

"This is for punching Deva," Yudhraj said as Diyohan started bleeding.

He advanced and landed another punch, "This is for making me punch the old lady."

Before Diyohan could block his next attack, Yudhraj grabbed Diyohan's armour and with all his strength threw another strong punch at him, it connected with Diyohan's jaw and damaged his chin.

"And this one is for the touching Drupa."

The last punch was very strong, his grip on the armour was so firm that it broke. Diyohan couldn't stand on his feet as he was punched repeatedly on his face. He got a little dizzy and tried to maintain his balance.

Diyohan failed to stand and fell on the ground.

He tried to get up as quickly as he could.

"Stay down," Yudhraj said as he placed his foot on Diyohan's broken armour.

Arjun Vs. Virakanna

Arjun looked at Virakanna, he observed his foot movement and started calculating the speed of his attack.

Virakanna held two thick, long and sharp swords in his hands. He stretched his hands wide open and ran towards Arjun.

Arjun charged towards him too. He moved his hand towards the bow and his arm lit up. He pulled the string and shot an energy arrow.

Virakanna was astounded to see this, using the presence of his mind he drew one of his swords upwards and

defended himself. The sword turned black due to the energy but remained intact.

Arjun stopped running and stood at a place and shot back to back arrows at him. He shot arrows with great accuracy and rapidly, it appeared as if they all were shot at the same time.

Virakanna used both his swords and deflected few arrows and dodged a few.

Arjun pulled the string as another arrow was formed; Virakanna was just a feet away from him. Arjun leaped over him. He placed his right foot on the shoulder of Virakanna, used his shoulder as a base and front flipped above him. While he was in the air and even before he could complete his motion, he quickly shot another arrow towards Virakanna.

Before Virakanna could realize, the energy arrow had blasted on his wrist. The shot was so strong that it totally damaged his right hand.

Arjun landed on his feet and looked back at Virakanna to find him on his knees, grunting.

Virakanna grabbed something from his coat and threw it towards Arjun. Arjun tried to pull the string again but couldn't find the time to launch the arrow. Virakanna threw a sphere towards him that exploded in mid-air, and numerous small arrow heads were launched towards Arjun.

Arjun jumped over to his left and ducked the attacks.

"That was close," he whispered to himself.

Virakanna reached out to his coat and pulled out a circular edged disk and threw it towards Arjun, he dodged it again. He looked at Virakanna to see what his next move was.

Arjun heard a swishing noise and turned back to see what was it. He found that the disk came back with even greater speed and it was just a few inches away from his face. Arjun quickly blocked it with his bow. The disk cut through his bow. He looked at his broken bow and threw it away.

Even with just one eye and a damaged hand, Virakanna had a great aim and confidence to fight. Arjun found him worthy enough and gave him a moment to get back on his feet.

He tore his coat and wrapped a piece around his palm.

"Your suit gives you the added advantage to fight; you think I didn't notice that?" Virakanna said as he held his wounded hand.

"Yes, it does," Arjun said as he picked up the arrowhead that was lying on the ground and threw it towards Virakanna.

And suddenly there was a huge sonic boom and a shockwave rushed down the sky, breaking some part of the roof of the royal court. The debris of the roof fell on the ground.

The impact of the shockwave hit the ground and a huge force erupted.

Chapter 22

The Alpha

Everybody had their eyes glued to the sky, even before they could figure out what was happening Arjun was hit with a blast. He dodged it, but the blast hit the ground just a few inches away from him. The force of the impact was strong enough to throw Arjun off the ground. He quickly looked at the sky in utter disbelief and shock.

"How is this possible? Sonic boom? Shockwave and lasers, here?" Yudhraj exclaimed as he looked at Arjun.

"I have no idea."

Nakul looked at the sky and saw the sun; he saw something diving towards them. The sun was bright and nobody could figure out what it was. Arjun kept looking at the sky, hard enough to get a sight of what was coming.

It was a man who dived straight towards them.

He was far away as he glided through the air, without anything.

Suddenly a couple of more lasers were shot and even before Arjun could move, all of them were attacked.

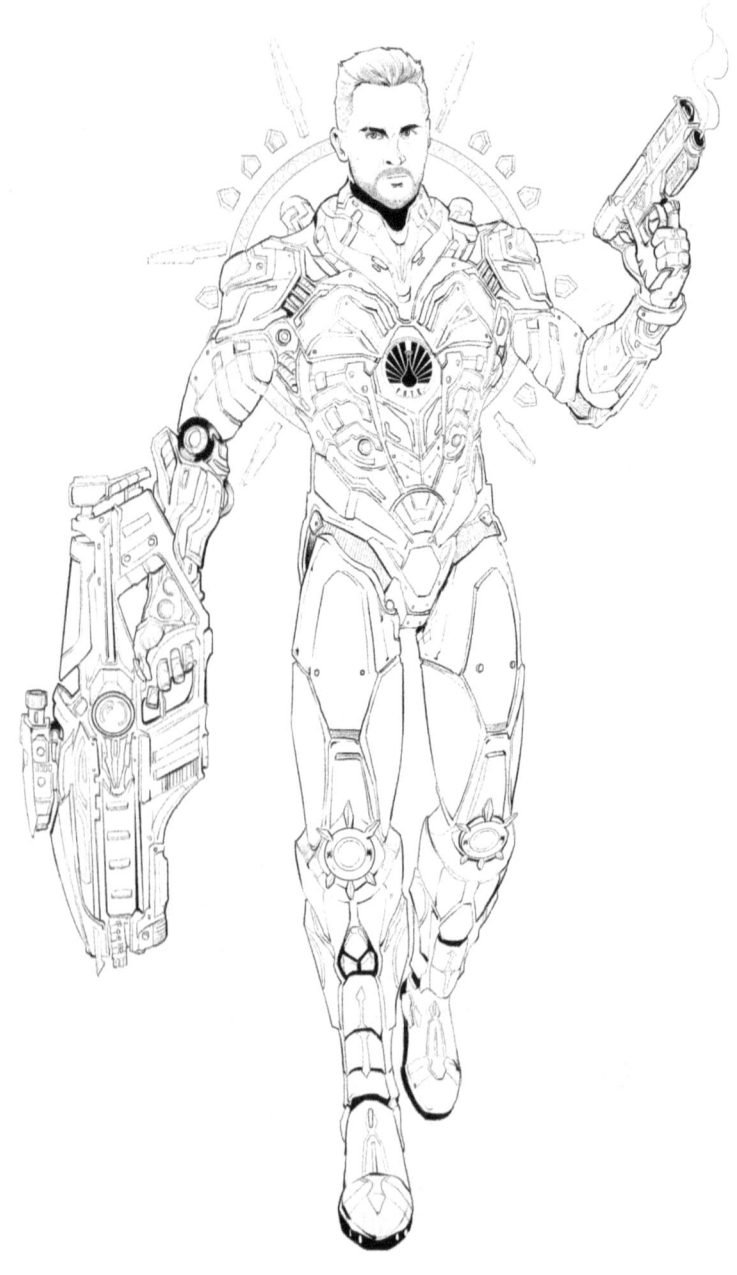

All of them fell on the ground and their suits had massive damages, and they were covered with bruises.

Diyohan looked at Virakanna and asked, "Who is he? Any of your assassins?"

"No, he doesn't belong to my force," Virakanna replied as he held his bleeding wrist.

The man was just a few feet above the ground and within a second he landed on one knee. His fist punched the ground and the dust around him made it difficult to see his face.

Everyone could only see his silhouette.

The dust settled and everybody got a clear view of him.

It was Karan!

Arjun grumbled as he saw Karan standing in front of him.

Karan's eye met Arjun's, and he said, "You criminal!"

Yudhraj looked at him with his eyes wide open and exclaimed, "What? Karan? How did you come here?"

Karan looked back at him and said, "Am I too early for the party? This doesn't look like the war I was supposed to intervene. But as long as I get to hunt you all down, I am good."

"What the hell is wrong with you? What are you doing?" Arjun asked as he approached Karan.

"Please! Maintain distance otherwise; I would be forced to put you down," Karan said as he pointed his sonic blaster towards him.

Karan looked around and found the King.

"King! You need not worry anymore! I have come to fight on behalf of your sons," Karan said in a loud and dominating voice.

Nakul ran towards him and said, "Man! Differences aside, you are going to support them? That's not fair!"

Karan looked at Nakul and said, "Fair? You fight these men with your advanced technology and talk about being fair? Get the hell away from my face."

He walked towards the five brothers and stood in front of them; he looked at Diyohan.

"You lost to these pricks? These guys? This is a team of dysfunctionals who got lucky," he said as he turned towards his former team.

He pointed towards Bheem and said, "A man who cannot control his inner beast."

He then moved his finger towards Yudhraj, "The leader who failed his force."

He looked at Nakul, smirked and said, "A being who possesses the powers of Gods but wasted his life in drug abuse."

He looked at Deva "This guy! A book worm."

And finally, Karan looked at Arjun, cleared his throat, and said, "Ah! The Great Arjun! Who has no honour, no rules and is the epitome of insecurities.

"You lost to them? These men?" Karan said as he laughed.

Karan looked around and found Bhishmaji and Dronaji.

"What? You wouldn't welcome your Alpha, or are you intentionally avoiding me so as to not hurt Arjun's sentiments?" Karan yelled and questioned Bhishmaji .

Bhishmaji looked at Dronaji and asked, "Is he talking to me?"

Karan turned towards Kison and said, "You have my respect, but it's about time we make this a fair fight."

"I choose to be on the sides of the princes and pledge to give everything I have to defeat the Heroes of Wars. I will fight till my last breath or until I kill all of them," Karan yelled out loud.

There was a pin drop silence in the courtroom.

Everyone stared at Karan as he took the oath.

The tables were about to turn!

The Alpha had arrived.

Chapter 23

The Fair Fight

K aran are you out your mind?" Yudhraj exclaimed.

Karan looked back at him and said, "To hell with you, Captain Yudhraj," as he emphasized on the word 'captain'.

"We are on a mission assigned to us by the organization, you cannot interfere in an ongoing operation," Yudhraj replied to his taunt.

"Oh, yes, the organization. I have fought my way here just like I have done since that lucky bastard came into the academy from nowhere," he replied as he glared at Arjun.

Arjun dusted the dirt off his armour and went walking towards Karan; they both looked right into each other's eyes. Arjun stood in front of him.

"Make a move and you shall regret it forever," Arjun muttered.

"Give it your best shot," Karan replied with a grin.

"You know, none of your weapons can cause any harm

to me," Karan said as he steadily clocked his blaster that was placed on his waist.

"Why are you doing this?" Arjun inquired.

"You are cheaters. This mission should have been aborted the very moment you got to know that this is an inter-time mission where the targets do not have the same level of weapons."

"For how long are you going to play by the fair and unfair rules of yours? These men are not even humans..." and Arjun was interrupted by Karan.

"Cut it already, I am going to defend them, all of them."

"And how exactly are you planning to do that? By standing in front of them with your Armour of Invincibility on?" Arjun asked with a tone of mockery.

"Oh yes, jealous since the day one of my armour. Aren't you Arjun, the one who earned the Galaxy Bow?" Karan replied with rage-filled eyes and disgust.

"Galaxy Bow? I left it behind the day I quit F.A.T.E, I am amused to learn that you haven't taken over the ownership of it yet."

"I don't feed on leftovers Arjun, I have pledged to kill you and then use the Bow," he replied.

"You are a greedy man; you already wield the world's strongest armour. Nothing can penetrate that, even with the deadliest attacks you will survive and you are still after the Bow?" Arjun asked him.

"Because I deserved the Bow more than you. I was

eligible and yet you got it just because someone thought you could put it to better use," Karan yelled out.

"Accept it, Karan, I was better than you," Arjun replied.

Yudhraj walked near them as he knew this situation was going to get worse if he didn't intervene.

"Relax boys; we all need to talk with an ice pack on our heads. We are on a mission assigned by F.A.T.E," he said as he placed his hand on Karan's shoulder.

He pushed away Yudhraj's hand and said, "I faced a hard time trying to convince the authority to let me make a time leap, I am not going to let this pass."

"But how did they allow you to make a time leap?" Yudhraj inquired as he was aware that the highest authority of the F.A.T.E had assigned them this mission and no way they can let Karan intervene.

"They didn't," he said menacingly.

Arjun had a slight grin on his face, a sense of satisfaction was evident, "Well that, makes you a fugitive. Just like me."

"How dare you compare yourself with me, you criminal!" Karan replied and punched his face.

Arjun lost his balance but quickly maintained it.

Before Arjun could attack, Yudhraj pushed both of them away from each other.

"Stop fighting; you are not in the academy anymore! Look where you are, understand the situation," Yudhraj yelled out.

The five brothers were standing there cluelessly as they saw the men from the future arguing amongst themselves.

Diyohan turned around at his brothers and said, "This seems to be the perfect opportunity to strike them, let's attack and finish this."

Dushalya, who was twisting his moustache while trying to comprehend the situation, quickly interrupted his brother and said, "No! Look at them. This new guy seems to be one amongst them but against them. We failed, but this guy shattered them with just one strike. If we want to win against them, we got to have him on our side."

Dushalya had made a strong point here, Diyohan seemed convinced.

"Okay then, the enemy of our enemy is our friend," Diyohan said.

He went walking towards Karan and was accompanied by Dushalya.

"Maha-Yoddha Karan," Diyohan addressed him with a cheerful voice.

Karan instantly turned around as he heard his name.

"King Diyohan," he said and touched his chest with his fist.

Listening to the prefix before his name, Diyohan was happy and filled with pride.

Dushalya took a step closer to Karan and said, "Maha-Yoddha Karan, we are glad to have your support on our side; you seem like the strongest of all. You made a remarkable entrance here."

Karan was being appreciated for his skills, something he rarely experienced. He looked at Dushalya with a twinkle in his eyes.

"Thank you," He replied.

"Maha-Yoddha, fight by our side. We will fight against these men; we will fight as brothers," Dushalya said.

"I offer you my loyalty and support until I die," Karan said in a loud voice.

Yudhraj looked at Arjun as he saw how things were getting out of hand.

"We cannot defeat them if Karan fights on their side. Arjun, we have to do something now," he said.

"With his invincibility armour everything we have is useless, he can literally stand in front of us and take all our attacks without any efforts," Arjun said as he knew fighting Karan wasn't easy.

Deva was quiet for a while, as usual, he was trying to figure things out and find a solution to end this problem.

"Hey buddy, you got something cooking in your brain?" Nakul asked as he poked Deva's head twice.

"No, I have nothing to say, but I think this is not it. It's not just Karan we have to be afraid of. If he has decided to come here, he must have studied everything about them and this world. He has an added advantage of knowledge with him," he replied as he moved away from Nakul who kept on poking his head.

"This is bad, very bad. He knows my weakness too. So

I am not going to fight him either," Nakul said as he scratched his head.

Yudhraj and Arjun regrouped with the rest of them.

" Bheem, if things get ugly, you will have to transform. Don't worry about us we will maintain distance from you," Yudhraj said as all of them stood in a circle.

"Arjun, you handle Karan and rest of us will take care of the other brothers."

Deva interrupted as he said, "But we don't have any more weapons. Our armours are damaged and we cannot fight with them in this condition."

"We don't have an option," Yudhraj replied.

Arjun abruptly left from the discussion and walked towards Karan.

Diyohan whispered something to Karan and he instantly turned around and was ready to fight Arjun.

"Come on let's have one round, you and me! This time you have no teacher to interfere and stop the match while you are getting beaten," Karan said as he tried to mock Arjun.

"You talk about fair fights? Look at us. We don't have our weapons; we don't have armours, we have nothing with us right now. Do you want to fight unarmed men? If that fits in your book of morals then yes, lets fight," Arjun replied.

Karan took a brief pause as he heard Arjun. He monitored everyone's broken armours, placed his blaster on his waist and was at ease.

"To be honest. I did a bit of research and took a time leap; however, I am a bit early. That doesn't change anything. The huge war is about to happen, but today is not the day. I don't want to murder you while you are unarmed. I will meet you at the battlefield and I will kill you, Arjun Sinha," he said as he looked right into his eyes.

"If not today then someday for sure, we will fight and this time I won't hold back Karan," Arjun replied.

Nakul tapped Yudhraj's shoulder repeatedly and said, "Do you think this was part of his plan or this happened by fluke?"

Yudhraj giggled and said, "Arjun and Karan are more or less the same, but Arjun has been on the streets and also to every corner of the unknown galaxy. He has a little more smartness than Karan, I believe. This has to be his plan."

"Smart," Deva muttered as he appreciated Arjun's brain.

Arjun stood in front of Karan looking right at him and both of them had a grin on their face.

"Done! See you on the battlefield," said Arjun and returned. As he came back walking, he shared a smile with Yudhraj.

Karan turned back at Dushalya and said, "Don't worry, everything is under control. He thinks he stopped me from destroying him, but he just postponed it and made things worse for them."

"What is your plan? How do we fight them? We see they have weapons we aren't aware of," Dushalya asked.

"As I said, don't worry. I have a little surprise for you guys too," He replied.

Dushan too joined the conversation as he heard his two brothers talking to the man from the future.

"Can you give us the weapons they have? If so, can we trounce them," he said.

"No, you don't have to use the weapons of the future. They have few limitations, but this era has the weapons of Gods and Demons. They are lethal; I know where to find them. So we will use them," Karan said as he touched few keys on his gauntlet and a holographic map popped out.

The map was huge; he pinched the hologram and resized it.

All the brothers were amazed to see this, Virakanna waved in the projection and his hand went through it.

"This is interesting; how do you do this?" he asked.

"Well, that's thousands of years for you to figure things out but forget that, let's focus on the map," Karan said as he pointed towards the red blinking spot on the map.

"This map shows the location of the Weapons of Destruction, however I am not aware of the Weapons of Gods. Given your history, you can wield demonic weapons better, I believe," He added.

"Weapons are my things, nobody knows better about them than me," Virakanna said with a sense of pride.

"Of course, I know that. So you and I will go there to get these weapons. While the rest of the brothers will stay here, done?" he asked Virakanna.

Virakanna nodded in agreement.

Karan turned towards Yudhraj and yelled out from a distance, "Take your time, this is going to be an interesting fight!"

Yudhraj did not react as he knew they weren't in the position to fight now.

Karan lifted his hand slowly and pointed a finger towards the sky.

"Look up, surprise! Heroes of Wars!" he yelled out loud.

Everyone at once looked at the sky. There was nothing, and suddenly a translucent patch was formed above them.

Deva's jaw dropped as he looked at it.

"No, no, no! If it is what I think it is, then we are doomed," he whispered to himself.

The translucent patch became darker and it turned out to be a huge aircraft hovering above them.

The ship safely landed in the lawn of the palace. It was bigger, it was highly equipped and the doors were gigantic. Unlike Archisa, it had multiple doors. One of the doors fell open with a thud. It was dark inside, just a few moments later, a loud roar came from within the ship and was followed by various screams and terrifying sounds.

Kison came back running to the court and stood right next to Deva.

Deva looked at him, asked, "You know everything, right?

How are we going to fight this now?"

Kison felt helpless; he looked at Deva with a downward gaze and said, "This is not how it was supposed to be."

Karan marched towards his ship. He was about to reach when he stopped in the midway and turned around. He cleared his throat and he observed everyone was staring at him. On his left side stood the five brothers and on his right were the Heroes of Wars, in front of him were the people of Yugprasth who looked at him with curiosity and shock. Every single person there was either clueless or scared.

With a very commanding voice, he said-

"Ladies and Gentlemen, may I present you THE BEASTS FROM THE FUTURE.."

TO BE CONTINUED IN PART 2- Heroes of Wars And The Beasts From The Future.